FIC
BOY   Boyd, Candy Dawson
         Charlie Pippin

DATE DUE			$12.95
OC 01 '04			
NO 04 04			
MR 14 '07			

Charlie Pippin

Charlie Pippin

Candy Dawson Boyd

Simon & Schuster Books for Young Readers

This novel is a work of fiction. Names, characters, places, and incidents are either the product of the author's imagination or are used fictitiously. Any resemblance to actual persons, living or dead, events, or locales is entirely coincidental.

SIMON & SCHUSTER BOOKS FOR YOUNG READERS
An imprint of Simon & Schuster Children's Publishing Division
1230 Avenue of the Americas
New York, New York 10020
Text copyright © 1987 by Candy Dawson Boyd
All rights reserved including the right of reproduction
in whole or in part in any form.
Simon & Schuster Books for Young Readers is a trademark of Simon & Schuster

The text of this book is set in 12½ point Berkeley Old Style Book.

Printed and bound in the United States of America

First Edition
10 9 8 7 6 5 4 3

Library of Congress Cataloging-in-Publication Data
Boyd, Candy Dawson.
    Charlie Pippin.
    Summary: Spunky eleven-year-old Charlie hopes to understand her rigid father by finding out everything she can about the Vietnam War, the war that let him survive but killed his dreams.
    [1. Fathers and daughters — Fiction.   2. Vietnamese Conflict, 1961-1975 — Fiction.   3. Afro-Americans — Fiction]   I. Title.
PZ7.B69157Ch 1987   [Fic]   86–23780
ISBN 0–02–726350–9

For my husband, Robert Boyd,
and my father, Julian Dawson

Charlie Pippin

One

Chartreuse "Charlie" Pippin scanned the early-morning sky. Perfect Berkeley, California, weather—clear and blue. Good business weather. She grinned as she counted out change. At the same time, Charlie watched for Mr. Rocker, the principal. Making money at Hayden Elementary School meant taking risks.

"Okay, kid, that's two pencils, sharpened, with new erasers for seven cents each. Your total is fourteen cents. Here's six cents change," Charlie said, pressing the coins into the palm of a smiling third-grade boy.

"Thanks, Charlie. I'll lose discipline points if I don't have two pencils for the test," he said.

"Yeah, I know. If you win the trip to Disneyland, remember I was the one who helped you. Plus you saved six cents and a lecture by buying from me instead of the office." Charlie thrust a receipt stamped CHARLIE PIPPIN into the boy's hand.

A straggling line of eleven children stood behind the portable classroom on the east side of the schoolyard. "Next," Charlie said. With her usual efficiency she took orders, handed out pencils, collected money, made change, and wrote receipts.

By the time the school buzzer rang, Charlie's gray metal change box bulged with coins. Quickly she locked the box, shoving it, along with her supplies, into a battered briefcase. She swung a purple bookbag over her right shoulder, and she ran. Being late was only *one* of the sins you could commit in Mrs. Hayamoto's sixth-grade room.

Charlie dodged past clusters of students. Starting a new school year with a new teacher unnerved her. She knew that some teachers liked her, and some just didn't. Her big sister, Sienna, on the other hand, always got teachers who adored her. Her father said it was because Sienna was good and that Charlie should act more like her.

Barely scooting in before the classroom door closed, Charlie caught her breath. She'd gotten one tardy yesterday, and she'd already lost points on Mr. Rocker's Discipline Code contract. Her father wouldn't like that.

As soon as the morning attendance had been taken, the sixth-graders settled down to their achievement exams. These covered reading, math, writing, and subject areas like science and social studies.

Charlie hurried to finish, skimming the pages and marking neat black bubbles on the computer answer sheet. After turning in her test, she propped up her desk top with a social studies book. From a lavender plastic pouch she took brightly colored origami paper, one of her grandmother's paper-folding instruction books, and a small, sharp pair of scissors.

Schoolwide testing would end in one day. After tomorrow the demand for her pencils would plummet. But the little girls, bless them, would eagerly purchase the crisply folded paper penguins, birds, and sharp-nosed dogs. The best-sellers—puffy goldfish and rabbits—would disappear like pecan pancakes from her father's plate. Some girls built collections to play with.

Charlie grinned to herself. If the boys liked the paper samurai hats and warriors, she might even have a boom before Halloween, which was when she usually did her best business.

Charlie's fingers moved deftly, folding a red paper square that was white on one side into the basic origami balloon shape. In seconds she would blow through a tiny opening. Like magic, a red paper rabbit, complete with ears, would puff to life, ready to hop about. Charlie smiled, remembering the July afternoon when her grandmother, Mama Bliss, had plunked her down in a chair and taught her how to make the Japanese paper shapes called origami.

A brisk recess run on pencils crowned Charlie's morning. Even the stash of old pencils she'd scrounged from the school grounds and sold for a nickel apiece evaporated. Confident that she could get pencils from her grandfather's store at a hefty discount, she promised a fresh supply the next morning.

Back in the classroom, Charlie lifted the top of her desk to experiment with a long samurai hat. A two-color combination of gold and red would be striking. The room was noisy. She looked around. Mrs. Hayamoto was trying to get thirty-one sixth-graders settled. It would take at least ten minutes for the math lesson to start. More than enough time. So Charlie began her work.

"What are you doing, Chartreuse?"

Charlie stared up at Mrs. Hayamoto's tight face, wondering how someone so young and pretty could look so mean. "Folding quietly until math starts," she said, not taking her black eyes off the teacher.

"Put that away and get out notebook paper. Write two hundred times, 'I, Chartreuse Pippin, will concentrate only on my schoolwork.' And you'll take a note home this afternoon. I want the note returned tomorrow morning, signed by both of your parents."

"You're not being fair, Mrs. Hayamoto. What was I doing wrong?" Charlie stood up. Four thick ponytails swung from side to side as she tossed her head back. Charlie's cheeks, the same color as Jell-O chocolate pops, flushed with embarrassment.

Out of the corner of her eye Charlie caught Katie Rose Bainbridge's sympathetic smile. From the depths of a book, Chris Saunders peered up. They both sat at her cluster. There were four kids in each of the other groups jammed around the classroom, but only three in the one Charlie was assigned to. They were wedged in the far corner of the room near the windows.

"I was only making samurai hats, not talking or bothering anybody." She turned to her classmates. Chris nodded. Katie Rose bent her head.

"Chartreuse, that's not the point. According to the Discipline Code, you are supposed to be engaged in schoolwork all of the time, be a—"

" 'Responsible learner.' I know all that. But you weren't teaching us anything."

"Don't talk back to me. Get busy, Chartreuse."

"My name is Charlie. I don't like Chartreuse."

"And I don't have time to learn nicknames. Kathryn Rose, pass back the math tests. Get to work, Chartreuse," snapped Mrs. Hayamoto, her eyes flashing.

By lunchtime Charlie had reached two conclusions. Number one, Mrs. Hayamoto didn't like her, which meant she was in for a rough school year. Number two, she'd have to be more cautious with her business.

Charlie ran up and stood by her line partner, Katie Rose. Ignoring the hubbub of the lunchroom, the girls claimed a table and sat down. Hesitantly, Charlie opened her briefcase and took out her lunch. No telling what Sienna had fixed, especially after their argument last night.

Sienna, her fifteen-year-old sister, fitted into Charlie's life like a splinter, the kind that pushed in deeper and deeper with each attempt to yank it out. Last night Sienna had accused her of taking some hair clips. Charlie figured the green polka-dot clips were inside a pair of shoes on Sienna's half of their bedroom, which resembled a junkyard.

The aromas told Charlie that her sister was after real revenge. Lunch was bologna on white bread with gobs of mayonnaise and sweet pickles. Digging into the bag, she found a package of cheese-flavored corn chips. No red Rome apple. Not even one carrot stick.

Across the table, Katie Rose unwrapped her sandwich. Charlie couldn't resist staring at the sprouts on whole-wheat bread with cucumbers and Swiss cheese. She wanted to snatch the bag of carrot sticks and that perfectly symmetrical pear.

"Want to swap?" Katie Rose's blue eyes were warm and friendly. "I'm staying at Mom's now. She's writing a book on healthy food that kids can fix. Charlie, stop drooling. Here. I hate healthy lunches."

"And I love them," said Charlie, gratefully handing over her paper bag. They laughed. This was the third time she'd eaten with Katie Rose. "But now that Mama has Sienna making lunch for me, I don't think I'm going to have any."

"I love bologna and steak and hamburgers," Katie Rose said between happy chomps.

"I try to keep to a vegetarian diet," said Charlie. "But I eat beef, chicken, and fish sometimes."

"Why would you diet that way?"

"My uncle Ben is a vegetarian, so I decided to try to be one, too." Charlie chewed slowly.

"What do you do with the money you make?"

"Save some. I buy jewelry with the rest. See?" Charlie touched a shiny purple and blue beaded necklace.

"But why do you have a business, especially at school?" Katie Rose persisted.

"I've been making things and selling them since I was in second grade. My first product was paper birdcages. Then I made greeting cards." Charlie crunched on a carrot. "I just love having a business."

Katie Rose shook her head. "I guess I'm a coward. Getting caught would make me stop. That's if I got up the nerve to start in the first place."

"Mama Bliss, my grandmother, sells bottles she paints. She says that being a businesswoman is part of my West African heritage. Those women ran the marketplaces."

"Too bad you're at Hayden instead of in West Africa," said Katie Rose.

Charlie stopped eating. "Look, I know that selling stuff

at school isn't exactly right, but it's no crime. I'm not doing anything that corrupts minors. But when my father sees that note, I'm going to be in terrible trouble."

"Yeah, we're here at Hayden to be 'responsible learners,'" quoted Katie Rose. "My old school was nothing like this place."

Charlie remembered that Katie Rose had transferred in only last week. The one good thing Mrs. Hayamoto had done, she thought, was make Katie Rose her line partner.

"That Discipline Code is tough." Katie Rose popped a corn chip into her mouth. "If you try to keep your business going, eventually Mr. Rocker will find out. And with the Code he could put you out of school!"

Charlie nodded. "You're right. I think I can get around Mrs. Hayamoto, but the principal is a problem. If I can just stay out of his way, I'll be okay."

Mr. Rocker, the principal, enforced the school policy. All children and parents had to sign a contract that listed rules of good conduct ranging from completing all homework to keeping a neat desk. Students who obeyed earned points as "responsible learners." The thirty children with the highest total by June would win a trip to Disneyland in Los Angeles. Charlie sighed. Her chances of getting to Disneyland equaled her chances of getting along with her father. Zero.

"Katie Rose, my daddy believes in that Code like some people believe in the Bible. He's a law-and-order man. I am not exaggerating when I say he'll kill me over that note. And my mama will just stand there and say, 'Oscar, don't be so hard on Charlie. She'll outgrow this stage just like all the others.'"

"At least your father and mother live in the same house.

I had to get my father to sign the contract, then call my mother, bike over to her apartment to get her signature, bike back, and answer all of my father's questions about what my mother was doing. Running back and forth between the two of them is a hassle."

"Don't you live with your mother?"

"I'm a joint-custody kid," Katie Rose explained.

"What does that mean?"

"I live with my father four days of the week and with my mother three days. It's supposed to keep me well adjusted and stable."

"Are you?" Charlie asked, sinking her teeth into the pear, then licking at the sweet juice running down her chin.

"No. I'm tired of forgetting to pack the books and clothes I need. They store everything in different places! Mom threw her iron out. Dad can't even find his. Look at me."

Charlie did.

"Go ahead and laugh." Katie Rose wore gym shoes with no socks, a black sweat shirt that said CONDEMNED PROPERTY, and a wrinkled orange cotton skirt. Her straight, dark brown hair was parted in the center, falling on both sides of her face and below her shoulders. "I call this outfit 'joint-custody punk.' If this school had a dress code, Mr. Rocker would send me home."

"Which home?" teased Charlie.

Across the long and narrow lunchroom table, the girls grinned at each other.

Back in the classroom, Charlie took out a newspaper. History and current events fascinated her. Each day she took the leftover newspapers from her grandfather's grocery store home to read. She turned to a story she had started about a Black Vietnam War veteran who had given the six medals he'd won for heroism to his teenage son. Charlie knew that this year marked the tenth anniversary of the end of the longest war Americans had ever fought—and the only one we'd lost. She shivered, remembering the coldness in her father's eyes when she'd brought up Vietnam at dinner last night. Her father was a Vietnam vet, but he wouldn't say a word about the war, except when he and Uncle Ben argued.

On the front board Charlie noticed a list of topics for current-events projects. Mrs. Hayamoto was writing student names beside each heading. The list included the African famine, South Africa, medical issues, local news, children's news, world leaders, the national deficit, entertainment, and war and peace. Charlie found her name. She was in the entertainment group.

As soon as class started, Mrs. Hayamoto read off the topics and names. "Now the last committee, Christopher, Kathryn Rose, and Michael. Your current-events subject is war and peace."

"Mrs. Hayamoto, I don't want to be in entertainment. I want to be in the war and peace group," interrupted Charlie, waving her hand in the air. "I want to report on the Vietnam War."

"Why?" her teacher asked. The class waited while Charlie sat there, silent.

Charlie struggled, surprised at her sudden demand. She knew why she had to choose that topic. Yet how could she tell her teacher in front of the whole room that she had to be on the war and peace team so she could learn about the war her father had survived. And her favorite relative, Uncle Ben. Then maybe she could find out why her father wouldn't talk about it.

"Because I'm more interested in that issue than entertainment," Charlie said. "Please, Mrs. Hayamoto, this is important to me. Plus this year is the tenth anniversary of the end of the war."

"I don't want to be in that war group," said Michael. "Entertainment is more my speed."

"All right. But I expect outstanding work from both of you, since you're so interested in these topics," Mrs. Hayamoto said with the hint of a threat in her voice. "Remember, this report is sixty percent of your social studies grade for the term."

After the teacher explained the purpose of each committee, adding directions for working together, she allotted time for the students to think about their projects. Then she told the children to meet with their teammates.

"Let's move closer." Chris Saunders plucked a mechanical pencil from behind his ear and tossed it to Charlie. "Do you know how to use one of these? You take notes."

"Yes, I do. And what do I look like? Your personal secretary? You can write, can't you? You take notes." Charlie tossed the pencil back to him. If there was anything she resented, it was getting bossed around. She got enough of that at home from her father and Sienna. Chris Saunders was no smarter than she was. He wasn't going to get away with telling her what to do.

"Peace. Remember, this is a war and *peace* committee," said Katie Rose. "So I'll act as secretary today. Chris, you can take the job next time. Then you, Charlie. Fair?"

The two nodded.

"Who wants to start? Mrs. Hayamoto said that we have to state our individual project goals. Chris?" Katie Rose took a pen from her desk.

"And, Chris, please talk in short, simple sentences, not long paragraphs," Charlie added. Chris had a terrible habit of talking more like a teacher than a student.

"Come on, Charlie, we'll never get started if you two keep this up," said Katie Rose.

Chris cleared his throat. "First, I plan to collect current data sources on wars around the world. Next, I'll construct graphs and charts. Finally, I will share my results with the class," he said. "Is that short enough?"

Katie Rose held up both hands. "My turn. I want to learn more about nuclear war and the protest movement. My brother is a protester, and he has a lot of information."

"That leaves you, Charlie," Chris said.

"I want to find out about the Vietnam War. About how the grown-ups who fought in it feel about war ten years later. And what kids know about that war."

Chris rolled his eyes.

"Okay, Mister Know-it-all, tell me, where is Vietnam located?" Charlie leaned back in her seat.

He frowned. "Somewhere near Russia?"

Charlie laughed.

"No, I don't think so. Near India, right?" asked Katie Rose.

Charlie shook her head as she opened her newspaper and pointed to a map. "You are both one hundred percent wrong! See!" She showed them the part of the world called

Indochina and Vietnam, a long, snakelike, S-shaped country that sat on the South China Sea, bordered by China to the north and Kampuchea (formerly Cambodia) and Laos to the west.

Chris sneered. "Who cares? Vietnam happened a long time ago."

Charlie grinned. "Exactly when did the war begin and end?"

"I can answer that one!" Katie Rose said. "If this year is the tenth anniversary of the end of the Vietnam War, and the war was ten years long, then it must have started in—"

Chris interrupted. "1965."

"Most people think it started on March 5, 1965. That's the date the first United States Marines landed at Da Nang," Charlie said.

"Who cares? My dad was an airborne trooper. He says that rehashing what happened in Vietnam is a waste of time." Chris tapped his mechanical pencil. "And that the parades and memorials are ten years too late."

"There's been a lot about it on television. I don't like to watch all that shooting and killing," Katie Rose said.

"Did your father fight in Vietnam?" asked Chris, leaning toward her.

Charlie watched her friend's ears turn red.

"No. He couldn't pass the physical exam because of a heart defect. Anyway, we have to decide what we'll have done by the next time we meet." Katie Rose stammered as she said it.

"Mine did, Chris Saunders! And you can write this down with your fancy pencil: I'm going ahead with my idea. I don't care if you think it's important or not," Charlie declared in such a loud voice that Mrs. Hayamoto turned her head.

Chris and Katie Rose stared at Charlie. Charlie looked away, wondering if they could work together on a project that meant so much to her.

Two

After school, with the note from Mrs. Hayamoto jammed in her pants pocket, Charlie placed her briefcase in the bike basket, snapped on her safety helmet, and pedaled off. She enjoyed riding her bike the three blocks to the small grocery store with red trim. Over the screen door was a sign that said PIPPIN CONVENIENCE STORE.

"Hi, Granddad," Charlie said, rolling her bike to the rear. Quickly she parked it in the back room, beside the stairs that led up to her grandfather's neat apartment. Then she went to the counter to help him wait on the school-children stopping by. Spying four boxes of Number 2 pencils under the counter, Charlie smiled.

In about forty minutes the store emptied.

"So how did school go, Granddaughter?"

Her grandfather was a tall, gentle man. Everything about him was ordinary, except for two things: the way he talked—in questions—and his eyes. Hawk eyes, shot with gold, blinked and settled on her face. Charlie decided to ask for supplies first, then tell him about her project.

"I sold all of my pencils. I need more. Could you give

me a good break on the price, Granddad?"

"Don't I always? You're not getting into trouble again, are you?"

"How did you know?" Charlie asked, squiggling her stubby toes inside her shoes.

"Don't I always?"

Charlie dug into her pocket. Silently she handed the note to him.

His eyes moved over the sheet of paper. "Uhmm. Uhmm."

"That bad, huh?" Charlie took the note and put it back. Out of sight, out of mind, she thought. She wished that were true.

"What do you think your father is going to do? Is he out of town on business?"

"Nope. What can I do?"

"Shouldn't you take your medicine?"

"Will you sell me a dozen pencils so I can fill the orders I took today?" Charlie perched on one nervous foot, biting her top lip.

Granddad wore his usual white shirt and gray tie under a maroon knitted vest. Even though he and Mama Bliss had been divorced for six years, they acted like married people. Charlie knew Mama Bliss still knitted the warm vests for him, and he continued to eat Sunday dinner with her. Charlie bit harder.

"Chartreuse Pippin, where did you drift away to? Now, listen to me, if I sell you those pencils, what is going to happen?" Not waiting for an answer, he went on, "Don't you think you'll end up in more trouble with your father?"

"But, Granddad, I promised my customers pencils!"

15

"What have I been trying to tell you?" he asked.

"No."

"Now, you go on home," he ordered.

"Oh, Granddad, I have so many orders for pencils. Think of the profit I'm going to lose." She ran her fingers over the smooth glass beads around her neck.

"What do you think your father is going to do when you bring that note to him and you are late getting home?"

Without another word, Charlie dashed for her bicycle. All of her plans to tell her grandfather about her Vietnam War project wheeled out the front door with her. Left behind were the day's newspapers. All she could think about was facing her father.

The frantic ride home took Charlie less than fifteen minutes. The house her family lived in was located on the south side of the University of California–Berkeley campus. Charlie loved her quiet street, nestled below the green hills.

Sienna was standing on the porch with their father as Charlie wheeled up. "Shoot! Both of them are laughing. Goody girl Sienna must have done something wonderful again," Charlie muttered to herself as she lugged the bike around the one-story house to the backyard.

Hearing Popcorn's yelps helped. "Stay back, Popcorn," Charlie ordered the cream-colored Lhasa apso. She unlocked the back gate and leaned the bike against the redwood fence. Then she sank down onto the ground and gathered him near.

"Hi, you ragtag dog. What've you been up to today?" Charlie asked. He yapped at her and scrambled out of her arms and over onto his back, so that his short legs were raised in the warm September air. Popcorn's head lolled to one side in contentment as Charlie scratched his stomach.

"This is where I want to stay, right here in the yard, just me and you, Popcorn. No Mrs. Hayamoto. No bossy Chris Saunders. No Mr. Rocker. And no Daddy or Sienna."

Near the back fence loomed a large rock. The first time Charlie saw it she announced to the family that there was a star in the backyard. The sound of her father's scornful laughter still stung. But Charlie knew that chunk of dark gray rock was a hunk of star that had fallen from the sky. Why not? At the top of her star was a niche that made a comfortable perch.

The fresh smell of the grass failed to hide Popcorn's doggy odor, reminding Charlie that he needed the bath she'd promised him days ago. "Popcorn, tonight, if I'm still alive, I'll give you a bath."

"Hey, Charlie, get in here! You better wash these morning dishes so we can start dinner," yelled Sienna from the back door, letting Sheba, her Siamese cat, out.

Jumping up at the sound of Sienna's voice and the sudden sight of Sheba, Popcorn shook himself and growled. Popcorn and Sheba tolerated each other much the way their owners did. Reluctantly, Charlie dragged herself up the seven back steps.

"Hurry up, Charlie. I have to go run with Daddy. You are as slow as molasses."

Long, wavy hair, the same burnished copper color as their father's, framed Sienna's light eyes, tinted with flecks of gold. Her sister had inherited their mother's creamy brown color and high cheekbones. Always, for as far back as Charlie could recall, Sienna had been the "beautiful" one. Mama kept telling her that she made Sienna a lot prettier in her mind than she actually was. But Charlie didn't pay attention to that.

"I'll wash and cut the broccoli. You grate the cheese over the chicken casserole. And this time make sure you do the casserole exactly the way Daddy likes it," Sienna said. "Use lots of cheese, not the two tiny dabs you put on last time. Honestly, Charlie, sometimes I think you want to make him mad at you."

"And what if I prefer to wash the broccoli? Mama didn't say anything about me obeying you," Charlie said.

Leaning against the kitchen counter, Sienna pursed her full lips. "If Mama Bliss was here, she'd say that you look like death warmed over. Have a bad day at school, little sister?" Sienna liked to emphasize the last word in every sentence, an affectation she'd borrowed from a soap opera star.

"Wrong. My day was great." Charlie spoke in low tones. "I got special permission to do a report on the Vietnam War. I'm going to interview Daddy, Granddad, and kids at school. And write Uncle Ben. I'll talk to Mama Bliss if she's in a decent mood. And Mama."

"Then why are you whispering? Afraid Daddy might hear you?"

Charlie knew that her father was changing into his running clothes.

"Because young ladies don't yell," Charlie retorted, quoting him.

"You're finally getting some sense! I wouldn't bring up Vietnam to Daddy. You know how he is. You really want to clean the broccoli?" Sienna drummed her fingernails on the counter.

"Nope. I see you found the hair clips you accused me of stealing."

"Yeah. Under my bed. I bet that dumb, dirty dog of yours put them there."

"He's smarter than you are! And he won't be dirty after I bathe him tonight. Oh, yeah, thanks a lot for that slop you fixed for my lunch."

Ignoring Sienna's laughter, Charlie went to check on her father. She tiptoed past the bedrooms, the one bathroom, and into the dining room with the wooden set-in drawers. She could see her father in the living room, stretching by the fireplace. His bad leg shook visibly as he strained forward.

Moving backward, Charlie paused before entering her bedroom. Her bed was next to the door. In the far left corner, under a low window that looked out over Charlie's hummingbird feeding cage, was Sienna's bed. Each sister had her own desk with four bookshelves above it. Mama had put up the shelving. With separate chairs, wastebaskets, and chests of drawers, the room was as crowded as Charlie's sixth-grade classroom at Hayden Elementary.

Charlie laid her bookbag and briefcase on top of her neat desk. Later she would total her earnings and stash them in the locked cashbox beneath her bed, next to her watercolor paints and brushes.

With the air of a connoisseur, Popcorn surveyed the

piles of Sienna's clothes before him and sank upon the softest one. Charlie grinned. "Good for you, boy. Sienna would die if she caught you and your fleas on her blouses!"

"Charlie, didn't you hear your sister calling you?" said her father, standing in the doorway.

"Sorry, Daddy." In unison she and the dog jumped, together meeting her father's impatient face. "Want some company today?"

"Sienna's running with me, and you have to clean the kitchen." His thick black mustache shifted up, then down.

Charlie's face drooped.

"When you're older you'll be able to keep up. Now you'd just slow us down."

"But I could try, Daddy."

"You're not good enough yet. Sienna wasn't ready to join me until last year. She never complained the way you do," he said, shaking his head in disapproval. "Why are you always in such a hurry to tackle things you aren't ready for?"

Meeting his eyes, Charlie stiffened inside. Her father was a big man, over six feet tall, with broad shoulders and large hands. When he spoke in that booming bass voice, she tensed.

Abruptly, he hollered for Sienna and left. Moments later, the front door locked behind them, leaving Charlie alone. In her pocket, she felt for the note, wishing it would vanish.

Grating the cheese was relaxing, Charlie decided as she stood in front of the kitchen window. A quiet half hour passed before she heard her mother's measured footsteps.

"Hi, sugar. Those two out training for the Olympics?" Mrs. Pippin set a grocery bag down on the round kitchen table.

"I asked Daddy to take me. He always says I'm not ready yet. But, Mama, I know I could keep up with them," said Charlie.

"Sugar, stop beating your head against a stone wall, and I mean your father. You know how he is. He'll let you run when he's ready and not one second sooner," she said. "I'm going to change and take my meditation break. You are cordially invited to join me, Miss Chartreuse Marie Pippin." Mama held out her arms.

Welcoming the hug, Charlie leaned back and kissed her mother's soft, dark face, which was ringed by softer curly hair cut close. Large and lush, Eleanor Pippin was a stunning woman.

"Mama, you know I can't sit still for five minutes! Maybe tomorrow." She moved back.

"Promises, promises. That's all you give me," her mother teased, sorting through the mail. "I spend my life checking bills." Mrs. Pippin worked in the billing department at a children's hospital.

"Mama, there's something I should tell you," Charlie said suddenly, realizing her father and sister could return any second. "Mrs. Hayamoto made me write two hundred lines and bring a note home for you and Daddy to sign because I was making some origami hats. But she hadn't even started the math lesson."

"Were you supposed to be doing math?" Her mother stepped out of her high heels and bent to pick them up.

"No, Mama, she was trying to get the rest of the kids quieted down. She said I should have been studying. She's not fair! I wasn't bothering anybody."

"Charlie, you know that school is not the place to make origami things. Is it?" Mrs. Pippin held her forehead. "This means an argument with your father. Does she have to have his signature?"

"Yeah. Mama, Mrs. Hayamoto doesn't like me."

"Why not?" Sienna stood in the kitchen, slightly out of breath, Mr. Pippin behind her.

"None of your business," said Charlie, her face reddening. Popcorn's ears perked.

"I need something cold to drink. We got any orange juice, baby?"

Oscar Pippin moved past Sienna, kissed his wife, took the note out of her hand, and collapsed into a wooden chair. Charlie picked up Popcorn as Sienna leaned over her father's shoulder and read the note aloud.

"You're getting off to a great start this school year, aren't you, Charlie? Everybody is pulling their load in this family but you! Your mother is working long hours. I'm flying all over the Northwest checking supervisors to make sure their auto insurance claims are accurate. Sienna is doing well, like she always does. And you? What are you doing? You are eleven years old! When are you going to start acting like it?" he yelled.

Charlie retreated to the stove. She hated it when he hollered at her. Especially in front of Sienna. Sometimes she thought that the more he traveled as a claims manager for a large automobile insurance company, the more he yelled at her.

"Put that stupid dog down! And don't open your mouth! I don't want to hear anything you have to say. Give me a pen, Eleanor." He grabbed the pen and signed the note, then handed it to his wife to sign.

"Daddy, I wasn't talking or bothering anybody."

He started to lunge out of his seat, but Mrs. Pippin quickly reached over and put her hand on his shoulder.

"Come on, Oscar, don't be so hard on Charlie. She'll outgrow this stage just like all the others."

Charlie held her ground. Her mother had acted true to form. She hoped her father wouldn't. The last time he'd gotten this mad, he had raised his hand to hit her. But stopped.

"I'm taking away your television privileges. You hear me?" He stood up, standing over her like the dark rock in the backyard. "You're just as irresponsible as that do-nothing uncle you love so much."

"Oscar, don't bring my brother, Ben, into this," said Charlie's mother, her soft face stiffening. She placed her other hand on Charlie's shoulder.

"A man comes home for a little peace, and look what he gets. All I want to hear from you, Charlie, is 'Daddy, I will obey the school rules.'" The bushy black eyebrows shot up as straight as soldiers at attention.

The silence in the kitchen created a roar of its own. The rubber band snapped back and forth in Charlie's stomach. Finally, under the weight of her mother's discomfort, Sienna's smugness, and her father's anger, she bent.

"Daddy, I'll follow the school rules."

"Obey!" he snapped.

"Obey," Charlie repeated.

During dinner, Aunt Jessie, Mama's older sister, called. She lived in Washington, D.C. Charlie listened to the conversation, hoping that her aunt would ask to speak to her. Today she was more than ready to accept her aunt's usual invitation to visit.

Pieces of talk told Charlie that Uncle Ben had left his job in Chicago and bought a camper. He had started for California two weeks ago, but planned to stop along the way.

"That fool," muttered her father, stabbing at a chunk of chicken covered with a thick layer of sharp cheddar cheese. "Ben is a fool. Jumps from one computer programming job to another. Lives like a sixties hippie."

"And he acts weird, Daddy," Sienna chimed in.

"No, he doesn't! Sienna, you wouldn't know weird if it walked right up and knocked you out." Charlie put her fork down.

"Shush," said her mother from the telephone. After several more minutes of clucks and "oh, dears," she returned to the table.

"That brother of mine is like tumbleweed, rolling from one spot to another. Oscar, Jessie says he's headed our way. Lord knows, I've missed him. Almost a year since we saw him."

"I haven't missed him," announced Sienna. "He could stay away forever."

"You and I see eye to eye there." Her father chuckled.

"I hope he comes here. I love Uncle Ben. He has the right to live his own way, Sienna. Why do you want everybody to be the same?" Charlie asked.

"You *would* admire Ben. He's got the sense of an eleven-year-old," retorted her father, winking at Sienna. "Seriously, Eleanor, I'm not sure I want him to stay with us. He's not a good influence on Charlie."

"Oscar, I don't appreciate your sarcasm. My brother is a fine man, even if he moves around a lot," she said, patting Charlie's hand and eyeing Sienna. "You know that war changed Ben."

Charlie frowned. Mama always referred to the Vietnam War as "that war," as if it didn't deserve a proper name.

"Number one, Eleanor, Vietnam ended ten years ago. The war is over. Done and over. Number two, I served there, too, in case you forgot."

"How could I forget, Oscar? Wasn't I waiting for you when you finally came home sixteen years ago? July 26, 1969, to be exact. That war changed you, too—and your dreams. Remember our old dreams, Oscar? I still do. Tell me, why are you so hard on my brother?" Mama waited.

"Ellie, giving up dreams for responsibilities is life, something Ben needs to learn," he snapped.

"Ben is part of us, Oscar. Family. We take family in," replied Mama. "My brother has never asked us for a dime. How he lives is none of our business."

Mumbling a hasty "Excuse me," Charlie cleared her place, grabbed her jacket, and took Popcorn out back. Sheba strolled behind them. The sun was setting. Shafts of rose, mauve, and pink light streaked the sky above.

Next door the lights lit up the Neilsons' empty kitchen. They were an elderly white couple who stayed to themselves.

Popcorn stretched out while Sheba stalked the shadowy

corners of the yard. From her place on the rock, five feet above the ground, Charlie spoke to Popcorn. "I wonder what Mama means when she talks to Daddy like that. They get so mad and sad when that war comes up, Popcorn." Charlie sighed. "I'm glad I made Mrs. Hayamoto let me do this project."

Popcorn barked.

"Uncle Ben will be here soon! You hear that, Popcorn? At least Uncle Ben thinks you and I are special."

Charlie thought about her father. He didn't like Uncle Ben any more than he liked her.

As the stars glittered in the darkening sky, Charlie shivered. "Popcorn, you need a bath, and I've got a hundred and twenty-eight lines to write. Should I make the origami rabbits tonight? I gave my word to some girls." Charlie inched down the rock and started toward the house.

Before she reached the back door, Charlie stopped to look at her father in the kitchen light. What did Mama mean about the Vietnam War changing Daddy's dreams? Imagining her father as a dreamer was impossible. He was a man of rules and responsibilities, not dreams.

Three

Charlie looked at the calendar on the wall behind Mr. Rocker's bald head. Friday, the thirteenth. Last night she had bathed Popcorn, written lines, and made origami rabbits. *And* clipped out two old magazine articles on the Vietnam War. Now she couldn't do anything except worry.

"Mr. Rocker, please don't call my father at work. Call my mother."

"You were breaking my Discipline Code. This time I caught you, right?" The principal was built like a beer barrel, with a face like a retired prizefighter's. He loosened his wide tie.

"Yeah, I know," Charlie said. The girls had been waiting, eager for the origami rabbits in her briefcase. When Mr. Rocker had plodded over to the back of the portable classroom, Charlie had been down to the last two bunnies. In her mind, she saw the girls scurrying off, leaving her alone.

"What am I going to do with you, Charlie?"

"Look, Mr. Rocker, I told those girls I'd have their

origami rabbits at morning recess. They paid me in advance. What could I do?"

"How about giving them their money back and putting up a Going Out of Business sign?" he replied. "Charlie, Hayden Elementary School is not your private corporation. Guess what? You are attending a public elementary school. You are a student, not a corporate whiz. Right?" He glanced at her student folder and began dialing.

"Mr. Rocker, this isn't the best time to reach my father. He's at a meeting in San Jose all day. Why not call him tomorrow?" she advised.

"Tomorrow is Saturday. Hello, I'd like to speak with Mr. Oscar Pippin. Mr. Pippin? This is Mr. Rocker, principal of Hayden Elementary School. Right. I'm sorry to disturb you at work, but I'm calling about your daughter, Charlie."

Feeling queasy, Charlie listened. Finally the conversation ended.

"Your father will see you at home." The principal stood up. "Now, Charlie, hear me. You sell anything else at my school, and I'll suspend you. No more warnings. Right?"

"Yes, Mr. Rocker."

"Why not win that trip to Disneyland? Be a team player. Follow the Code. Right?" He opened the office door.

Weak-kneed, Charlie returned to her classroom.

"What happened?" Katie Rose whispered when Mrs. Hayamoto's back was turned.

"Rocker called Daddy. At work. He told me that he'd suspend me if I sold anything else at school," said Charlie, shaking her head.

"What do you think your father will do?" asked Katie Rose.

"I'm too scared to think about it."

"Be quiet, you two. I'm trying to concentrate," said Chris Saunders.

Normally, Charlie would have argued with him, but not this afternoon.

Charlie worked at her grandfather's store until almost five o'clock. He had a sore throat and went upstairs after she arrived. At least she wouldn't have to tell him she'd gotten into trouble again.

When she got home and past Popcorn in the backyard, Charlie spotted her father. He was standing in front of the kitchen window, waiting for her.

"So, you disobeyed me again," he said after she closed the kitchen door.

Charlie inched away. Popcorn scooted behind the stove. The rage distorted his face, frightening her. Where was Mama? Or even Sienna? Sienna could make him stop.

"Do you have any idea how embarrassed I am? Being called at my job by the principal of the school because you don't know how to obey rules?"

When her father got this furious, Charlie put her hands over her ears. Still she could hear the words, name-calling words like *bad, irresponsible,* and the ones that hurt, *no good.*

"Don't you cover your ears! I'll knock those hands down!" Mr. Pippin threatened, so loud that Popcorn yelped.

Charlie jerked up and clasped her hands tightly. "Daddy, please," she said.

"Please, what?" He came toward her. "What kind of daughter are you? Why can't you behave like your sister?"

As he moved closer, Charlie backed against the stove. Her head pounded. "Please, Daddy!"

"Oscar, what in the devil are you berating this child for now? Stop hollering at her! I can hear you all the way down to the end of the block!" Mama Bliss stood in the kitchen, a set of house keys in her hand.

"Mother, this is none of your business. You may be renting me this house, but I'm the man here," he said.

"What happened, Charlie?" Mama Bliss asked.

"Mr. Rocker caught me selling origami rabbits and called Daddy." Charlie wiped at her nose.

"And you scream at her for something like that, Oscar?" Charlie's grandmother set her purse down. "The child wasn't lying or stealing or cursing folks out! I can recall dozens of times I sat in the principal's office because of some fool thing you'd done!"

Charlie watched her grandmother, a small brown woman with reddish hair streaked with white. Mama Bliss wore glasses. The frames had broken months ago. Somehow the screw that held the left side of the frame together had fallen out. A paper clip dangled in its place, serving as a temporary pin. With a firm shove, her grandmother propelled her out of her father's path. Then Mama Bliss laid her purse down and took off her thick sweater. "I'm going to make a pot of coffee. Join me, son?"

In the meantime, Charlie scooped up Popcorn. Sheba sneaked around the doorframe.

"Charlie, go to the bathroom and wash your face. Then I want you in your room doing homework," he ordered. "One more infraction like this and you'll lose every privilege you have! For the rest of the year!"

"This child is a lot like the child you were," said Mama Bliss, shaking her head sadly. "She's just full of life, Son."

Charlie was mad. Mad and hurt and hurt and mad. And when she thought about how her father treated Sienna, never raising his voice or calling her mean names, the anger bubbled out.

"You never treat Sienna like this!" she yelled back at him, amazed that such hard, hot words were leaving her mouth. "I wish Uncle Ben was my daddy. Not you! I hate you just like you hate me!"

Before he could react, Charlie scampered for the bathroom and locked the door. Behind the wooden door she heard shouts from her father and grandmother. Later, heavy footsteps pounded down the hallway, past the bathroom. The front door slammed shut. More footsteps followed. Charlie recognized her mother's and sister's. She knew Mama Bliss would let her alone for a while. Then she heard a knock on the door and a whisper. Sienna.

"Let me in, Charlie. Daddy's gone."

"What do you want? To laugh at me?"

"No. Open the door."

Charlie did.

"You okay?" Sienna asked. "What did you do this time? Rob a bank?" She stood before the mirror.

"No, I didn't rob any stupid bank! And if you're going to tease me, just leave!"

"All right, I'm sorry. But, Charlie, you've got to learn

that getting along with Daddy means one thing—doing what he tells you." Sienna touched her hair and face in the mirror. After patting Charlie's shoulder awkwardly, she left.

Charlie waited, then eased the door open.

"I hear you. Get that skinny backside in here, rebel," yelled her grandmother. The husky voice carried the length of the hall.

Mama Bliss sat in a kitchen chair scanning a horse racing form. In front of her was a cup of coffee. Like a thin, red bird she twisted her head and darted those sharp eyes about.

"You're spending your Friday night with me. Tomorrow we've got that crafts fair. Can't keep you tomorrow night because I'm heading up to Reno for three days with my bridge club," said her grandmother. "Ellie, try this coffee. Just like you like it. Strong enough to walk."

Charlie watched as her mother came over.

"You really had no business selling those rabbits. Your father did overreact, but you know better." She kissed Charlie on the cheek. A pungent, woodsy scent surrounded the kiss.

"Humph. There's a dead cat on the line, Eleanor. And you'd better wake up and smell it." The six white whiskers on Mama Bliss's chin bristled. Charlie knew her grandmother meant there was something wrong going on. "Lord don't like ugly, Daughter. Your husband is my flesh and blood, but treating children so differently is no good. I think what gets his goat so is that this one reminds him of what he used to be—full of dreams and daring. Seems like he lost that somewhere. And we know where."

"Mama Bliss! Let us handle this in our own way. And, Charlie, try to stay out of trouble with your father. I mean that," Mrs. Pippin said.

"How was Daddy different from the way he is now?" The question popped out before Charlie knew it. But she'd remembered her mother saying that the Vietnam War had changed her father.

Charlie's mother walked over to the kitchen window, her back to them. "Once upon a time your daddy would have been the first one to declare that your hunk of rock out there was a real star." She stood there. "Mama Bliss, you know it wasn't only that war that affected him. What happened afterward was just as bad. He and I had such wonderful dreams! We were going to buy some land and start our own inn. The hours we spent planning how we'd have four children and raise them in a beautiful, wild place on the Oregon coast. I would write poetry and he would—" Abruptly she stopped.

Charlie stood still, hoping to hear more. Her mother had started to tell secrets never shared before.

"He would what, Mama?" asked Charlie, seeing a signal pass between her grandmother and mother. She knew that Mama loved her father in a deep way far beyond her ken. Often the privacy of the feelings between them left her out.

"Nothing. Nothing that matters now. Old dreams die." But when Charlie examined her mother's face, she saw tears in her eyes.

Mama Bliss cleared her throat. "Sorry, Eleanor. I'm not trying to interfere in your family. But each year my son gets more rigid and more strict with this child. Somebody's got to fix this." Taking off her glasses with little regard for the broken frame, Mama Bliss rubbed her eyes.

"I don't want to discuss this. Too much has been said here." Mrs. Pippin started out the door to the hallway. Charlie saw her mother's hands flutter by her sides in that light, trembling way of hummingbird wings.

"I'll close my tired eyes and squint. Maybe my prayers will get heard up there. What do I know, Eleanor? I'm an old woman with old bones for brains. Rebel, come on," she said, pointing a long finger at Charlie. "Get a move on. We've got bottles to pack to sell at the fair and a card match to finish."

"Can I take Popcorn?" asked Charlie, her head spinning from all that had happened.

"You know I can't stand dogs. Now get ready to go. We're on a tight schedule." Mama Bliss's head swooped down as she attacked the racing form like a robin snaring a juicy worm.

Four

The card table wobbled as Charlie arranged the bottles. Mama Bliss unlocked the change box. The Saturday morning sun shone bright, heating the tops of their heads and backs. Already crowds thronged the narrow paths between aisles of artists displaying their pottery, weaving, handmade clothing, bolts of brilliantly decorated cloth, drawings, stained glass, and more.

Charlie longed to find the jewelry vendors. There was enough money from the disastrous sale of the origami animals to buy something new.

Today Charlie wore enamel earrings shaped like rainbows, five strands of red and green glass beads, and seven bracelets. She paused to admire the bracelets on her arms, grateful for a grandmother who let her wear jewelry. Her father would get her for sure if he caught her wearing so much jewelry.

"Get a move on, Charlie. There's plenty of money to be made today. If the weather holds out, we could sell every bottle I brought. And you'll get your fifteen percent for helping me," said Mama Bliss, positioning herself in one of the two folding chairs.

"Sorry," said Charlie, aware that her grandmother was still miffed because she'd lost at cards last night. They hadn't talked any more about the confrontation in the kitchen. Part of Charlie wanted to. But now was not the time, she thought, as two customers stopped at the card table.

Her grandmother's painted bottles sold well. Each year Mama Bliss selected a different theme. Charlie's favorite had been the "ocean" year, when leaping porpoises, blunt-nosed whales, and exotic fish swam around the tall glass bottles. This was the "tree" year. In the bottles, people would place dried flowers, real floral bouquets, or candles.

An older woman, wearing a beret, bought a tree bottle in shades of green, yellow, and peach. The shellacked paint glistened in the light. While Mama Bliss chatted with her, Charlie wrote out the receipt, made change, and wrapped the bottle in newspaper.

Years ago Charlie had figured out that her grandmother wasn't on the crafts circuit for the money. She had enough of that from the houses she owned and the years of investing wisely with her ex-husband. Seeing her grandmother laughing and exchanging quips with all kinds of people, Charlie had understood the real reason they traveled from one local crafts fair to another: Mama Bliss relished the stimulation that came from being involved with others. She was curious about what people ate and who they voted for.

Charlie wrapped four bottles for a tall white man and added the two ten-dollar bills to the stack in the change box. She liked people, too—but what she was thinking about now was money.

At last the crowd thinned, and Mama Bliss took over while Charlie roamed the grounds. The fair was held in a park in the middle of Berkeley. There were tables where people could buy buttons and posters that spoke out against racism in the United States, apartheid in South Africa, nuclear war, sexism in the workplace, child abuse, battered women, and wars in countries around the globe. Charlie stopped at a table. She deliberated between two buttons. One said NO MORE VIETNAMS, the other WELCOME HOME, VIETNAM VETS. Unable to decide, Charlie handed over two dollars and pinned both to her sweat shirt.

Selecting a piece of jewelry took more time. Charlie was torn between a pair of ivory earrings shaped like flower petals and a silver ring with a green stone.

"Charlie! You're still alive!" exclaimed Katie Rose, coming out of nowhere.

"Katie Rose! Hi! I didn't know you liked crafts fairs," said Charlie.

"Come on and meet my mother."

Katie Rose introduced Charlie to a plump, freckled woman.

"You just bought one of my grandmother's bottles, Mrs. Bainbridge!"

"How did you know?" Mrs. Bainbridge asked, puzzled.

Charlie giggled. "Because when I wrap the bottles they look real neat, but when Mama Bliss does, she slaps masking tape all over the ends!"

"Mother, Charlie and I are line partners. We eat lunch together. See her buttons? We're on the war and peace team," said Katie Rose. She was dressed in the same outfit she'd worn on Friday.

They chatted for a while and parted. Charlie decided on the ring with the light green stone. She put it on.

On her way back to her grandmother's table, she paused to watch a face painter. The young woman was painting multicolored flowers on the face of a little girl, sprinkling the centers with gold glitter. Charlie knew how to do that. Mama Bliss had taught her last year.

After they sold the last tree bottle, Charlie and Mama Bliss packed the car and climbed in. The sun was low now. One glance up told Charlie why she had goose bumps. Waves of white fog were rolling in across the city and over the Berkeley hills. Charlie reached for a wool blanket on the backseat of the car. Except on rainy days, Mama Bliss drove the fire-engine-red Volkswagen convertible with the top down.

As they pulled up in front of her grandmother's house, Mama Bliss said, "Now let's unload the car. Then we'll grab a quick bite to eat while I figure out the profits and give you your cut. I've got to catch a bus to Reno tonight!" She hit the clutch, shifted into neutral, and braked.

"Mama Bliss, I need to talk to you about something," said Charlie.

"You have to talk while we work because I'm running behind schedule."

It wasn't until Charlie had accepted her commission and was biting into a toasted cheese sandwich that Mama Bliss stopped moving. "It's about what happened in the kitchen yesterday," she began.

"Get to the point."

"Do you think Daddy hates me, Mama Bliss?"

"I don't have time for psychology. Eat up! Of course

not! But what I think doesn't matter if you don't believe that."

"What about the rest?" persisted Charlie. "Tell me, what did Daddy dream of doing in Oregon at the inn?"

"No use starting that up. Best to leave all of that alone. You just can't understand what your mother was feeling about the way he used to be," Mama Bliss whispered, gazing away at the messy kitchen littered with half-dead plants and stacks of magazines.

"Do dreams have to die?" asked Charlie.

"Some of them just go naturally. Others get torn away. War kills dreams." In the weak late afternoon light, her grandmother's eyes seemed watery.

"Did any of your dreams die?"

"A few. Stop this dream talk. Chew!"

"I'm doing my social studies report on the Vietnam War. My teacher let me, so she must think I can learn something," Charlie said.

"Didn't mean to talk down to you, rebel. You can study facts about the war and read books and all, but understanding what happened to those young kids is a horse of a different color! Some of them were eighteen! Can you imagine sending someone barely three years older than that sister of yours off to some godforsaken jungle to kill or be killed?" Mama Bliss shook her head. "Insanity."

Charlie couldn't. Sienna couldn't find her way to Sacramento. "So you're telling me that my Vietnam project is a waste of time?"

"Clean your plate. Nope. What I'm saying is that reading books is only going to give you a certain kind of information. The rest has to come from people. Those who went there and those who waited for them to come home. And even when you have that, there's worlds you won't understand," said Charlie's grandmother, rinsing off the dishes, "especially what happened to our men. Hand me your plate."

Charlie obeyed, her mind humming away. Mama Bliss was right. She didn't understand much. But they weren't helping her by keeping these secrets. So she would just have to help herself.

"Charlie, you've got that look on your face. What are you plotting?"

"Just thinking about what you said." Quickly, Charlie changed the subject. "I'm glad you're not still mad at me for beating you at blackjack last night."

"Not as long as we start a Scrabble tournament the next time you come over. Now, when you get home, try to stay out of his way."

"I'll do my best."

Minutes later they were headed for Charlie's house. The hills were now blanketed in fog, and the memory of the laughter and excitement of the crafts fair seemed covered by the white misty air. As they got closer, Charlie bit her lip.

"I'd take all that jewelry off and those two buttons," said her grandmother as she swerved around a driver trying to park in a no-parking zone.

"Right," replied Charlie. "Thanks."

"How are you going to handle this Vietnam report? Delicately, I hope, and with prayer," cautioned Mama Bliss.

"I'm going to start my research at the library on Monday.

After I learn enough, I'll interview the family plus kids at school to see what they know. I thought if I was careful I could ask Daddy a few general questions. I hope you and Granddad will help me. And Uncle Ben's supposed to be coming soon, so I can talk to him," Charlie rattled on.

"Sounds like you're bound and determined to do this. Why?" The red Volkswagen swung down Charlie's street.

Charlie was busy taking off the jewelry and unpinning the buttons. Within seconds she'd stowed them away in her bookbag.

"It's something I have to do, Mama Bliss." Charlie thought about Chris Saunders's reactions to her project. "Deep down inside I believe that learning about the Vietnam War is important."

"To whom?" With a flourish, Mama Bliss pulled into a parking space in front of the house.

"Me." Then Charlie saw her father walk by the front window. "Can I go to Reno with you?"

"No reason to be scared, child. I'll go in with you, but only for a quick minute." Before getting out, Mama Bliss pulled one of Charlie's ponytails affectionately. "Chin up, rebel!"

Charlie's heart turned with the metal key. Daddy was in the small room off the living room, watching a football game. He looked at her briefly, then greeted his mother.

Charlie was relieved to hear the telephone ring suddenly. She kissed her grandmother good-bye and went to answer it. It was a boy named Joshua who wanted to talk to Sienna. He left his telephone number. She hung up. So Sienna had a secret boyfriend. Daddy wouldn't like that.

"Who was that?" her father hollered.

"Somebody named Joshua Morgan calling for Sienna." When he didn't reply, Charlie took Popcorn out.

By the time she returned the rest of the family was home. Sienna had bought a new outfit, a skirt and sweater. Twirling around, she swished past Charlie into their bedroom.

"Charlie, you and Sienna have a bedroom to clean," reminded Mrs. Pippin, nudging her husband into the kitchen. "Oscar, you help me put these groceries away."

Charlie followed Sienna and closed the bedroom door behind them. "Somebody called for you," Charlie said.

"Saundra again, I bet."

"Nope. It wasn't a girl."

"Charlie! Don't tease me. This is important. Who was it?"

"His last name starts with an M, and the last digit in his phone number is eight." Folding her hands behind her, Charlie rested against her Snoopy pillow and relaxed.

Sienna threw down the skirt and sweater and marched over. "Tell me. Tell me right now!"

Yawning, Charlie examined her short nails.

"Are you going to tell me? All right! What do you want?"

"You do the morning dishes the rest of the month. And stop accusing me of touching your junk. And stop fixing me garbage for lunch. And one more thing: Stop calling Popcorn bad names. And Uncle Ben. I don't want you to say one more mean word about him." Charlie smiled confidently. "One more thing. You let me interview you and some of your friends for my Vietnam War report."

"When I get my own phone and my own answering

service, you'll pay for this." Sienna was stalling, but Charlie wouldn't budge.

"I give in. Tell me. Who called?"

"Mr. Joshua Morgan. He wants you to call him. And I told Daddy when he asked me."

Sienna started twisting a strand of hair. "Oh, I can't stand it! Joshua called me? What did Daddy say?"

"Nothing."

The room got quiet. Both sisters knew that their father had ironclad edicts about boys. They couldn't call boys or even have male guests until they were sixteen. Charlie couldn't care less. At best, boys were a bother.

"I can't phone him back," said Sienna, dropping next to Charlie. "Do you have any idea who Joshua Morgan is? Of course not, you're not even in junior high school. He's a starter on the basketball team and a senior. I can't even call him back! I could die!"

"I could help you." Charlie smiled and turned on her side, making room for her sister to moan and wring her hands.

"What will it cost me? My life?" Sienna looked up.

"Nope, just keep your word and act nice to Popcorn, Uncle Ben, and me," demanded Charlie. "And help me with my project."

Sienna twisted a larger clump of hair. "The last thing in the world I care about is some stupid war that we couldn't even win! You'd better not embarrass me in front of my friends with this silly report of yours!" she said. "I give up. Help me."

"All you have to do is call Saundra. Tell her to call Joshua. Here's his number. I wrote it down for you. Tell

Saundra to call Joshua and tell him that you can't call him, but you'll meet him early Monday morning at school."

"Charlie, you are so smart!" Sienna jumped up as the telephone rang again. Charlie followed her.

Mrs. Pippin got there first. "What is this, some kind of telephone convention?" She chuckled. "Hello? Oh, Ben, where in the world are you? That close! Wonderful. In about two hours? Now, drive carefully and take your time. See you soon."

Later Charlie heard her parents arguing about Uncle Ben's coming. Like a broken record, her mother kept saying, "Ben is part of us. Family. We take family in."

Charlie went out to sit on the front steps with Popcorn and waited for her uncle. Just as her feet became numb, a new blue camper drove up, the horn honking in rhythmic bursts.

"Uncle Ben!" yelled Charlie. In seconds she was swung up into the arms of a short, bearded man. His eyes sparkled like champagne bubbles.

"Charlie! My favorite girl! And Popcorn! Hi, fella." Uncle Ben was dressed in corduroy slacks and a combat jacket. On his belt hung a Swiss army knife and a calculator.

Mrs. Pippin ran out to hug him while Mr. Pippin and Sienna remained near the front door. Charlie tensed.

"Hello, Ben. Need any help with your bags?" called her father, his large frame filling the doorway.

"No, thanks, Oscar. I can handle everything." Uncle Ben smiled slowly. "Good to see you, man."

"Come on in. Sienna, say hello to your uncle," Mr. Pippin said.

Charlie shot her sister a glare, reminding her of the promises made earlier in the bedroom. She watched her father and Sienna come down the front steps. Her father's hand was outstretched, and Sienna had slapped on a smile.

Charlie let out her breath. She'd been fingering the Vietnam buttons in her jacket pocket for good luck. Maybe Daddy was finally going to act nice to Uncle Ben, and this visit would be different.

Five

Charlie made sure she sat next to Uncle Ben at the kitchen table. Seeing that he didn't have a napkin, she sprang up, squeezing past her father and Sienna. Mama Bliss should be here, Charlie thought. She would tell them to get those boards out of their drawers!

"So, Ben, you quit another job? Got any plans?" Mr. Pippin leaned back in his chair.

Charlie bit her top lip.

"The company folded, Oscar. My boss, Hank, offered me a limited partnership in his new consulting firm."

"Why, Ben, that's wonderful! What will you be doing?" Mama placed a plate of spinach quiche and salad in front of him.

Out of the corner of her eye, Charlie saw Sienna stop filing her nails.

"I had to refuse him. Living on airplanes and working twenty-hour days is not for me," he replied. "This is delicious, Ellie."

Sienna let out a loud, lengthy sigh.

Uncle Ben smiled. "Guess that means you're disappointed in me, Sienna."

Charlie spoke up. "No, she's not!" She kicked Sienna hard. Sheba snarled.

Uncle Ben patted his firm stomach. "Charlie, how's life been treating you?"

"Fine. Both of my friends from last year moved. Lucille to Seattle, Washington, and Johari's family went back to Atlanta. We weren't best friends, but they were nice. There's a girl I kind of like, Katie Rose Bainbridge. We're working on a social studies project," Charlie said. "I have to interview the family, Sienna's friends, and kids at school."

"What's this project about?" her father asked, frowning.

Charlie hesitated. "War and peace."

"Daddy, Charlie chose to report on the Vietnam War," interjected Sienna, her cat eyes glowing.

Mama spoke up. "Oscar, isn't your football game on?" But she was too late.

"What in the world can an eleven-year-old girl need to know about Vietnam? You can't begin to understand what happened there!" Her father straightened up.

"Oscar, hold on a minute. Maybe if we had been better educated about the issues, you and I wouldn't have lost our youth in Vietnam." Her uncle's deep brown eyes met her father's, unafraid. "And our innocence."

"Daddy, I think your game has started," Sienna said.

Like a bear scenting attack, Mr. Pippin swerved to the man across the table.

"Ben, Vietnam is over, and the sooner you realize that the better off you'll be!"

"And the sooner you realize that you're still fighting that war, the better off you will be," Uncle Ben said.

Charlie flinched as her father slapped his hand on the table.

"You've been running away ever since they flew you back from Vietnam. Dropping in and out of jobs. I feel good about going to Vietnam! It was a question of Indochina turning communist. We had to be there to stop that," he thundered.

Charlie knew the rest of the argument by heart. Whenever her uncle came, the two of them got into that war. But seldom in this angry way. Daddy always said that Presidents Truman, Eisenhower, Kennedy, and Johnson had been right about helping any countries threatened by communists. He argued that the United States had to go to Vietnam to help the people who lived in the south, the South Vietnamese, fight the Vietnamese who lived in the north, closer to communist China. If the South Vietnamese won, then communism wouldn't spread in Southeast Asia.

"Where was the support we needed to win, Oscar? The United States can't send men to be killed and maimed all over the globe helping other countries fight communism. We have too many problems right here!" said Uncle Ben.

This part was familiar to Charlie, too. Uncle Ben always disagreed. He believed that even if powerful countries like Russia and China had helped the North Vietnamese win, America and other noncommunist countries had no business entering a war they weren't really committed to winning.

Their argument made Charlie think of a crazy video game with huge nations shooting guns and flying soldiers to little countries to make them turn the same color they were. Red was for communist countries. Red, white, and blue for noncommunist. The winner was the big country that grabbed the most little ones. She knew her father believed that if the large communist countries won enough of the little countries, America would be in danger. She didn't know if that was true or not, but she certainly hoped not.

"Our country sent us to Vietnam, Oscar, and refused to give us what we needed to win! And now Vietnam is communist! So are Laos and Cambodia. I know, I know, just like the politicians said! But it's their own fault." This time her uncle was anything but calm. "At least those fat cats should have gone instead of sending mostly poor men and Black men to do the fighting and dying!"

Holding Popcorn tight, Charlie shrank. What was going on? Somebody had to stop this! Their kitchen was turning into a war zone!

"Oscar! Ben!" appealed Mrs. Pippin.

"I'll give you that, Ben. We didn't get the support to win. And I'll agree that the Black infantry soldier fought, was wounded, and died in Vietnam far more than was just or right. You have a point. Whites, especially those with money, those in college, got the safer, cushy jobs in the rear. Too many of them found a way to dodge going to Vietnam and a few of us, too, Ben." He pounded a clenched fist on the table. The plates clattered. "But if my country needed me tomorrow, I'd go!"

Uncle Ben sighed. "How can you fight for a country that doesn't respect you? Listen to me. Vietnam was a nightmare." His hands twisted. "You'll never convince me that you don't have any regrets about Vietnam."

Charlie watched her father's face constrict as if a powerful fist gripped his heart. Pain and sorrow flooded his eyes. For a second, she thought he was going to cry! He lowered his head. The kitchen got so quiet that Popcorn whined.

Uncle Ben spoke up. "I'm sorry, Oscar. I guess all that tenth anniversary coverage has gotten under my skin." He placed both of his hands on the table, flat, with the thick fingers spread.

Charlie wanted to pat the raised scars and deep grooves that covered his hands and fingers. The rubber band in her stomach was stretched as taut as a tightrope. Even Sienna looked scared, and her mother's head was in her hands. Still her father was silent.

"Look, man, I just do the best I can with what I've got. I try to be happy and not hurt anyone." Her uncle's voice, slow and soothing once more, washed over Charlie. "I'm sorry. Listen, I can stay in a motel. This is your house and I respect that, Oscar."

"No! No, Uncle Ben. Daddy, please don't make him leave," Charlie said.

"Oscar, why don't you go watch your game. Ben, you're not going anywhere. We're all family here, right, Oscar?" Mrs. Pippin got up and kissed her husband gently on his cheek. Without a word, he left the kitchen. Soon after, Sienna left.

Charlie, Mama, and Uncle Ben sat at the kitchen table. Popcorn lay on the floor. For some time they were silent, each gazing at a different spot in space. Charlie didn't know what to do. Suddenly her uncle stood up, saying that he'd bought something in North Carolina. When he returned, he carried a white paper shopping bag.

"Here you two go. Goodies for my girls!" He tossed the bag to his sister.

Mrs. Pippin began laughing as she dumped the contents. "Not buttons, Ben." She giggled, holding up a long strip of white paper covered with rows of green, yellow, and red candies.

To Charlie they looked like plump dots. She pulled a yellow button off and bit into the hard sugar. The three of them compared and then tasted the array of candies. Red and black licorice ropes. Fat, brown root beer barrels. Lemon drops. Sticks of cinnamon and blueberry. Golden butterscotches. Peanut butter cups. Orange corn candy with yellow tops. Peppermints. Crisp chocolates with green minty centers. Chewy caramels. Peanut brittle. Sugary orange slices. Taffy.

"Oh, no, Ben! I don't believe this! I haven't seen these since we were children," exclaimed Charlie's mother, giggling harder. In her hand were two white plastic forms shaped like Coca-Cola bottles, as long as the width of her hand. Charlie watched her mother bite off the top of one of the small bottles and drink the red fluid inside.

"Tastes just as sweet as ever. This reminds me of Mr. Slappy's store. You remember how you used to bribe me to buy you a big dill pickle and a peppermint stick to put in it?" Charlie's mother asked. "In return you promised not to tell Mother I put on her lipstick during recess."

Over the mound of candy, Charlie listened as her mother and uncle reminisced. Mama's face had relaxed. With Daddy out of the kitchen, the air seemed lighter.

51

She knew that spats between her father and uncle happened, but this one had scared her. It was hard to figure out which one of them was right about the war. Maybe her project would help her to understand.

When the telephone rang, Charlie answered, expecting Mama Bliss or Granddad. But it was Aunt Jessie from Washington, D.C., checking to see if Uncle Ben had arrived. Smiling, Charlie waited for her aunt's familiar litany.

"So when are you going to come and see me, Charlie?" she asked.

"Soon. Real soon, Aunt Jessie."

"You say that every time, and you've never been to visit me. Charlie, I know what a history buff you are! Imagine seeing the White House, the Lincoln and Washington memorials. Howard University, where I want you to go to college! And if you say, 'Oh, I'd love to, Aunt Jessie,' I'll come right through this telephone and get you!"

"Oh, I'd love to, Aunt Jessie! But this time I mean it."

They laughed. Then Charlie remembered her report.

"Aunt Jessie, I'm doing a special project about the Vietnam War. Isn't the Vietnam Memorial in Washington, D.C.? Have you been there?" she asked.

"Yes to both questions. But the Vietnam Memorial is not my favorite place."

"If I come, Aunt Jessie, would you take me there?" Charlie asked.

"I promise to escort you personally to the Memorial," replied her aunt. "Now, when can I expect to see you?"

Charlie giggled. "Don't be shocked if you look up and see me coming off a 747 jet airplane real soon, Aunt Jessie."

"Yeah, I'll believe you when I see you! Now, let me shout at my brother, Ben."

To Charlie's relief, Uncle Ben stayed. And the rest of the weekend and the bulk of the next week sped by. Eager to enjoy Uncle Ben in peace, Charlie made sure to stay out of trouble. No more origami sales. The briefcase remained under her bed next to the change box.

Two trips to the school and neighborhood libraries yielded only one book for kids her age about Vietnam. Fortunately the librarian let her search in the adult section. There she found one book about Black soldiers in Vietnam. And Daddy had bought a set of encyclopedias three years ago. But visits to her grandfather and time spent with Uncle Ben left Charlie without even a minute to look at the books.

On Friday morning, Charlie sashayed past Mr. Rocker and flashed him a big grin. Mrs. Hayamoto smiled at her when she entered the room. Chris Saunders was riffling through his bulging file of newspaper and magazine articles. He gave her a smirk. Charlie wondered if he knew how far behind she was.

"I'm going on a demonstration against nuclear war on Saturday," whispered Katie Rose. "Can you come? My mother could pick you up." Today Katie Rose wore two sweaters and a pair of jeans spotted with green paint.

"Daddy would never let me. I'd better try to get some— I mean, more interviews done," replied Charlie, feeling nervous.

"Charlie, how many interviews have you actually completed?" Chris peered at her over his glasses.

The honest answer was none. Last Sunday Uncle Ben had taken her to the Oakland Museum to see an exhibit on Black inventors. And this Saturday he'd promised to take her to the Monterey Bay Aquarium.

"I'm waiting. How many interviews have you completed?" Chris repeated, wrinkling his nose.

"Plenty. At least six," lied Charlie, ignoring Katie Rose's questioning look.

Taking a sheet of blue paper out of her briefcase, Charlie jotted down the things she had to do: Work on Vietnam. See Granddad. Call Mama Bliss and borrow some face paints. Start planning the Halloween business. Finish the list Daddy had given her before he went away.

The automobile insurance company that her father worked for had sent him to Portland, Oregon, until next Tuesday. Two mornings ago, distant and silent, he'd kissed her mother good-bye and driven to the airport.

At the end of the school day, Mrs. Hayamoto tallied the discipline points for each student on an official chart by the door.

"Are you joining the Discipline Code clique?" teased Katie Rose. "You didn't lose one point this week, 'responsible learner.' "

"I don't know," whispered Charlie. And she felt that there was so much she didn't know.

Six

That blustery Friday afternoon, the store was quiet. After about an hour, Granddad closed early. He was coughing and blowing his nose.

"You thought I forgot about your Vietnam report, didn't you?" He managed a weak chuckle. "Come upstairs while I get something for you and take my medicine. You know your grandmother made me vegetable soup? Have a bowl with me?"

That was just what Charlie needed. The one-bedroom apartment above the store with its waxed wooden floors and light-blue walls contrasted with Mama Bliss's large, cluttered house with rag rugs and peachy-red walls. Charlie wondered if that was why they didn't live together. Granddad couldn't stand a mess, and Mama Bliss had no patience for neatness.

A radio played jazz. Charlie recognized a tenor saxophone player whom both her father and grandfather listened to. Humming, she set out two ceramic soup bowls, spoons, and napkins. Remembering that Granddad ate wheat crackers, she placed several on a yellow plate.

"I'm glad Daddy is gone," she said aloud, arranging the crackers in two rows. "I don't think he loves me. Not like Sienna. I don't really hate Daddy. Maybe he loves me a little. Doesn't he?"

"Doesn't who love you?" Granddad asked. He was wearing a gray cardigan over his shirt and vest. He carried a magazine.

"Daddy."

"What makes you ask yourself that, Charlie? Here, you want to sit down?" He pulled out a chair for her and laid a *National Geographic* magazine on the table between them.

"He yelled at me last week and called me names."

"For selling that origami? Got caught, I heard. Your grandmother called me. Didn't know that, did you?" He sipped the soup while Charlie poked at a carrot.

"Uncle Ben loves me better than Daddy does, Granddad."

"Don't you want some of your grandmother's tasty soup?" He coughed. "Sounds like that red syrupy stuff is working, huh? Charlie, your father keeps pictures in his head. You following me? He tries to live life like a black-and-white photo album. No shades of gray. When you think about it, don't most of us? Try to keep things simple and manageable, I mean."

Charlie nodded. "Granddad, what did Daddy want to be when he was younger? I can't convince Mama or Mama Bliss to tell me. They say it's all old dreams, and old dreams die." Charlie waited. He was her last hope.

"You know what dreams are like, Charlie?"

She shook her head.

"Precious children. Some are frail, others strong from the start. And, like children, dreams are private. But why don't you ask him?"

"Because I'm afraid to." Charlie felt let down. "I guess you heard I told Daddy that I hated him."

"Have a cracker?" He coughed.

"Thank you, Granddad. I know Daddy doesn't love me like Sienna."

Granddad's eyes fastened on her. "Wouldn't life get monotonous if we all loved one another in the exact same way?"

"Are you thinking about the time he stayed with me, even at night, when I had pneumonia?" she asked.

Granddad smiled.

"And when I won the spelling bee and he called me the smartest girl in the world?" Charlie frowned, biting her lip. "But, Granddad, he's sweet to Sienna even though she never gets sick or wins any contests. All she does is say, 'Yes, Daddy. You're right, Daddy.' "

Her grandfather chuckled. "So what are you going to do? I've got one favor to ask. You listening?" He waited for her attention. "When you figure out how to make someone love you just the way you need them to, would you please come and tell me?"

The gold in his eyes dulled and a sadness crossed his face. Instinctively, Charlie kissed him, wondering whom he was really talking about.

"What's in the magazine?" Charlie reached for the *National Geographic* and read the cover. "The Vietnam War Memorial in Washington, D.C.? Aunt Jessie told me she doesn't like to go there."

He picked up the magazine. "I got this for you to take home. Use it for your project."

Curious, Charlie flipped through the pages and came to a photograph of a shiny black wall with thousands of names carved on it. A young Asian woman stood by the wall.

"Who's she?" Charlie asked.

"You read and find out. Now, finish that soup so I can take a nap. You get home. As your grandmother would say, 'I think I smell rain on the roof.' Don't you?"

The crisp smells of fall lingered in the late afternoon wind. As if eager witches and goblins scampered after her, Charlie sped home. Uncle Ben might be there.

The house was empty, except for Popcorn and Sheba. Sienna came in shortly afterward, and after spending an hour in the bathroom, rushed out the door. She was going to Saundra's for the night. Meanwhile, Mama had come home and gone to bed, complaining of a headache.

Then Uncle Ben came in. "Hi, honey! I had one of the best days a man could ask for! I had lunch with a good friend I haven't seen for a long time, and we ended up spending the entire day together!"

"Uncle Ben, could I interview you tonight for my report?" Charlie asked.

"Tonight?" His face went blank. "I've got to go out tonight. But we'll get together tomorrow. I promise." He started down the hall, singing.

"Where are you going tonight?" Charlie called.

In the middle of the hall, he did a little dance. "Out with my friend!"

"Are we still going to the aquarium tomorrow?"

"Let's take a raincheck on that. We'll go another time. Now I've got to shower, change, and get going." The singing started up again.

Stunned, she stood there. What was going on with him? Popcorn bounced after him, yelping. Charlie slammed her bedroom door shut. Sheba lay stretched across Sienna's bed, glaring at her. "You dumb cat! Get out of here!" But Sheba stayed. Charlie fumed. Then, not caring, she grabbed Sheba, jerked the door open, and almost threw the Siamese cat into her mother's arms.

"What's the matter with you? Why the tears?" asked Mrs. Pippin, pulling her robe close. "Hand me the cat, Charlie." She obeyed, and before her mother closed the door, she lowered Sheba gently onto the hall floor.

Charlie threw herself onto the bed.

"What happened?" her mother asked, turning on a light.

"Uncle Ben promised to take me to the Monterey aquarium tomorrow. And he broke his word to be with a friend," said Charlie, hitting her pillow.

"I just spoke to him. All that singing and door slamming woke me up."

In the soft light of the lamp, Mrs. Pippin's face was drawn as if pulled by invisible strings. Charlie flung herself close to her mother's body, breathing in the musky perfume, grateful for the strong arms that embraced her. She felt a hand rubbing her neck.

"Oh, Mama, I really wanted to go."

"Ben didn't mean to hurt your feelings. You know that."

"Who is this friend he has to see?" she asked.

"Dinah Sawyer. Your uncle knew her some time ago," explained Mrs. Pippin, changing positions so she could lie back against the pillows with Charlie in her arms. "Years ago, when he lived here for a while."

Charlie stared up. "You mean he broke his word to me to see—"

"His old girlfriend," finished her mother. "I'm glad he's dating Dinah tonight. She was good for him. I always thought they'd make a nice couple, but Ben got scared of making a commitment to her, so Dinah broke it off."

"He's been here less than a week and already he has a girlfriend. That's the last time I'll trust him."

"No, it isn't. Now, if you want to go to the aquarium so bad, I'll take you," she offered.

"Mama, why does Daddy get so mad at Uncle Ben? Because he does things like this?" Charlie asked, instead of responding to her mother's invitation.

"I'm so tired of refereeing those two! Keeping peace in this house is impossible." She closed her eyes, and Charlie heard the beating of her mother's heart. "Let's go order a pizza and curl up in front of the fireplace together."

"Can I interview you for my report?" asked Charlie.

"Sugar, I know this report is a big part of your social studies grade in school, so I won't stop you from doing it. But I've said everything I have to say."

"Okay, Mama."

"What about us going to the aquarium?" Mrs. Pippin asked. "You always turn me down for meditation."

The hush of the room calmed Charlie. Even Sienna's side was neat. On her desk she could see Uncle Ben's candy, origami penguins, a samurai hat, and a collection of rubber animals. Beneath the bed rested the briefcase, receipt books, watercolor paints, and change box. On the walls hung her posters from Mama Bliss of famous Black

60

women like Harriet Tubman and Mary McLeod Bethune. Her favorite was of Cicely Tyson, the actress. Charlie thought she was beautiful, like her mother.

Outside, the dark night covered her chunk of star rock. Somewhere the hummingbirds rested, sheltered from the wind. They didn't have to worry about Vietnam reports or uncles with girlfriends or fathers like Charlie's. She touched her mother's hair.

"So?"

Charlie could see the fatigue on her mother's face. Mama hadn't planned to spend a day driving the two to three hours to Monterey and back. She needed to rest.

"No, thanks, Mama. I need to work on my social studies project, plus Mrs. Hayamoto loaded us down with home-work." Charlie kissed her cheek.

"I love you, Charlie girl." She got up. "One magnificent vegetarian pizza coming up!"

"I wish Daddy could—" Charlie clamped her mouth shut, leaving the wish unspoken.

Mrs. Pippin stopped at the half-open door. Light from the hall streamed in.

"You know, Mama Bliss told me a story once about a little boy she knew who got so upset because the dog pound was rounding up stray dogs and killing them that he started a protest march." Her smile broadened. "He organized the children in the neighborhood, painted signs for them to carry, and had them walk up and down in front of the Humane Society. The police came, and there was a big write-up in the newspaper." She laughed.

Charlie stared at her mother. What was she going on about some little boy for?

"When he found out that his march didn't work, he

cut school to round up the stray dogs himself and hide them in his basement. He even sneaked money from his parents to feed them." She laughed harder.

Intrigued, Charlie asked, "Did he get caught?"

"Oh, you bet he got caught and got a good spanking! But Mama Bliss said that didn't stop him. He painted posters and tacked them all over town protesting the killing of the dogs. He even slept outside the dog pound with his sign!"

"What happened?" Charlie's eyes shone.

"I guess you'll have to ask your father!"

"Mama! Daddy would never do anything like that."

"Maybe you don't know your father as well as you think you do."

Later, with Uncle Ben long gone, Charlie and her mother sat before the fire eating a medium pizza spilling over with double cheese, tomatoes, black olives, mushrooms, green peppers, onions, and chunks of pineapple. Afterward, while her mother talked to a friend on the phone, Charlie made a reluctant decision. Time was running out. The challenge of interviewing Uncle Ben the next day spurred her to get up. She wanted to impress him.

Getting prepared meant examining the encyclopedia volumes in the family room, where Uncle Ben was staying. Daddy kept them on the bookshelf above the science fiction he enjoyed and Mama's spy books. In her bedroom, Charlie surveyed her research collection: two library books, one encyclopedia volume, one magazine article, and five newspaper articles! It was more than enough! Even Chris would have to agree.

Charlie arranged her green, pink, blue, and yellow index cards, pencils with new erasers, yellow legal pad, box of large paper clips, stapler with extra staples, ruler, and red ink pen. She plopped down at her desk and opened the encyclopedia.

After two hours of study, Charlie's head hurt. There was too much information to sort out. Weary, she reached for the green cards and began to list some general facts about Vietnam and its people. It was an old country, the size of California but with almost three times the population. Most of the people could read and write, lived in rural areas, ate rice and caught fish. But what really interested her was how long the Vietnamese had been fighting other countries as well as each other. Hundreds of years, she wrote, adding that China, France, and Japan had all tried to conquer Vietnam.

Forcing herself to skim the pages, on blue cards she jotted down dates and names that signaled important events that had led to America's involvement in a civil war thousands of miles away. Much of what she read she had heard her father and Uncle Ben discuss over the years.

Charlie picked up a pink index card and wrote down the costs of the Vietnam War, shaking her head in disbelief at the billions of American dollars spent. Thousands of people had been wounded or killed, and almost three million Americans had served there.

Except in the library book about Black Vietnam veterans, she found only two photographs in the rest of the materials that included them. But from listening to her family, she knew that thousands of Black soldiers had fought the ground war in Vietnam. Why weren't there more pictures of them? Not even one in the encyclopedia! It wasn't fair. Charlie resolved to ask Uncle Ben about it tomorrow.

Charlie was getting sleepy, but there was something she still needed to understand better—communism. Though she knew that the United States had gone to war in Vietnam against communism and thousands of people had died to stop it, she wasn't quite sure what it meant. And after hearing the word so much, it was high time she found out.

With a deep sigh, she trudged back to the family room for two more encyclopedia volumes. After a stop in the kitchen for a can of grape soda pop and a bowl of potato chips, Charlie rearranged the items on her desk so she could look up *communism*.

Forty-five minutes later she rubbed her eyes and stretched, surprised at what she had read. Over one third of the people in the world lived in communist countries, with governments quite different from the one she knew. It seemed that in communist nations like Russia, the government, or "state," owned the banks, transportation systems, even the newspapers, television stations, movie companies, and most of the land. Communists believed that by not allowing individuals to own corporations and businesses, life would be more equal for everyone. But, after what she'd heard from Daddy and Uncle Ben, Charlie wondered if all people in a communist country could really have the same good life. And she'd been disturbed to learn that people could vote only for the list of candidates selected by the government—and that they weren't allowed to speak out against the government.

Too exhausted to study more, Charlie decided that she'd have a tougher time having a business in a country like Russia than at Hayden Elementary School. She would research life in Russia later and get some books from the library. How could it be that people would want to live in countries where they had so few freedoms compared to Americans? But nobody would live there if things were that horrible, she reasoned, unless their ideas about freedom were different from hers—or they couldn't leave.

With that thought, she made herself write out a special list of interview questions for Uncle Ben. Then she brushed her teeth and fell into bed next to Popcorn.

Seven

Rough, wet licks woke Charlie. She squinted at Popcorn's furry face. He placed his left paw on her shoulder and pulled. Charlie knew what to do. She grabbed her robe and stumbled toward the kitchen to let him out.

The house was still. On the dining room table Charlie spotted a note in Uncle Ben's handwriting addressed to her mother. After reading the six lines, she tossed it down and jerked open the refrigerator. "He'll be with Dinah all day!" she muttered. "He won't be home for dinner! That means no interview!"

Charlie sulked despite her mother's efforts to comfort her. Finally, Mrs. Pippin left for yoga class—but not before waving the work list at Charlie.

First Charlie sat on the star rock watching Popcorn and Sheba. Finally, with a shake, she slid down and began her chores. The sun toasted her arms as she raked dead leaves into piles. Her jewelry tinkled in the air. Today she needed the comfort that came from wearing every piece she owned.

Just then Charlie saw her grandmother open the side

gate and enter the backyard. "So here you are, rebel. Decided to stop using my key. Seems to upset Oscar. I knocked and knocked. Rang that darn bell," announced Mama Bliss. She was wearing jeans and a sweater and a scarlet scarf tied around her head, the ends whipping about in the gusty wind. "You look like a gypsy, child. Who made you unhappy?"

"Nobody." At times like this, she wished that her grandmother was a touch senile. But Mama Bliss missed nothing.

"Charlie, don't you start answering me in those snapped-off, one-word retorts or I'll read your beads," said Mama Bliss, settling down on the third step from the bottom.

Charlie threw down the rake.

"Sorry, Mama Bliss." She sank down on the second step. "Uncle Ben broke his word twice so he could be with some stupid girlfriend of his. Mama left me with Daddy's dumb list to finish. I'm all confused about my Vietnam report, and it's sixty percent of my grade! Everybody keeps secrets from me! Nobody tells me anything!"

"Stop! First off, Ben's supposed to have a girlfriend," said her grandmother, standing up. "Oh, my heart is too weak for your foolish hysterics. Cage those beasts and grab a jacket. You're coming with me!"

"But I have to wash the dishes and vacuum and take out the garbage!"

"You've got thirty minutes! No more. Leave a note for your mother and put on those Vietnam buttons of yours. Old people don't have much time, so stop wasting mine."

Giving Charlie's ponytail two jerks, she started up the steps.

"Mama Bliss, can I please interview you for my assignment? You'll be my first interview," begged Charlie, holding the screen door open and being careful not to let Popcorn in. "I'm prepared! I have a tape recorder."

Thirty-three minutes later they were off. First stop was the Pippin store, where Mama Bliss dropped off more containers of soup. The kiss between her grandparents evoked the same reaction from Charlie that it always did—bewilderment. How could two people who loved each other so much stay divorced? Mama said that you could love somebody and not be able to live with them. Charlie had trouble figuring that out.

Loaded down with tofu, apples, granola, bran muffins, and papaya juice, Mama Bliss and Charlie left the health food store on University Avenue and headed for the University of California–Berkeley campus.

"We can't stay long, but I have a surprise for you," said Mama Bliss. The car was locked and the groceries safely stowed in the trunk.

Charlie wore comfortable clothes. In her backpack she carried her equipment. She slung it on her shoulder as they left the garage.

"What's going on?" asked Charlie. They were surrounded by hundreds of students as they tried to cross the street.

"There's a peace march today. We'll walk with them for a while, then double back here," announced her grandmother.

"But Daddy—" protested Charlie.

"What he doesn't know won't hurt him. How can you prepare a strong report if you don't have any real feel for what's going on?"

Grabbing Charlie by the hand, she pulled her into the moving crowd, next to a woman who had a newborn baby strapped to her. The baby, its round head covered with red fuzzy hair, turned and smiled at Charlie.

"Hi, I'm Helen Pippin," Mama Bliss said to the young woman with the baby. "And this is my granddaughter, Charlie."

After the introductions were completed, a new thought crept into Charlie's mind. Mama Bliss had planned this. She knew about the demonstration. That was why she'd told her to wear the buttons. And she knew it was the chance Charlie needed to interview people for her report.

Katie Rose was somewhere in the crowd. But Charlie couldn't run around searching for her. Not now.

Charlie turned to the pleasant woman. "I'm doing a report for school. Can I ask you a few questions, Sarah?"

"Sure. Go ahead, Charlie."

Out of the corner of her eye, Charlie caught a glimpse of the proud smile on her grandmother's face.

Quickly, Charlie got organized. She flipped open a small notebook, located some good questions, and dug out her battery-operated cassette recorder. The tape was in place. She depressed two buttons to record.

"This is Charlie Pippin at a peace demonstration at the University of California–Berkeley campus on Saturday, September twenty-first, about two P.M., interviewing Sarah Harris, who is . . ." Charlie paused. "How old are you, and what do you do?"

Sarah laughed. "I'm thirty-three years old, and I'm a librarian. This is my daughter, Jennifer Anne, who is six weeks old and a baby."

All of the demonstrators within hearing distance laughed.

"Thanks." Charlie held the built-in microphone close to her mouth and asked her first question. "Do you think the United States should have gone to Vietnam?"

"No. Now people are afraid of other wars like Vietnam getting started. I don't want Jennifer to grow up afraid of war, especially nuclear war, Charlie," said Sarah, her green eyes serious.

Mama Bliss added, "Children have a right to get old, like me!"

"Do you know anybody who went to Vietnam?" asked Charlie.

"My oldest sister was a nurse there. But my brother refused to be drafted and fled to Canada."

"You mean he ran away?" Charlie thought about the men in her family.

Sarah looked uneasy. "He was a protestor. Shush, Jennifer."

With a quick switch, Charlie changed the subject. "Last question, Sarah. Do you know anything about what war is like?"

Her face went blank. "You'll have to ask somebody else that question. I don't know. 'Bye, Charlie."

A gruff, hard voice plunged in. "You want to know what war is like, kid?"

Charlie stared up into the flat, light eyes of a white

man. In the background she heard Mama Bliss talking to someone else. Sarah had left with her baby. On the man's right arm a blue tattoo stood out against sandy-colored hairs. A cross on top of a heart.

"Sure." Charlie gulped. Only when her father fell into his private sadness did she see this same bleak expression.

"Imagine crawling through the bush and you crawl over some guy's leg. Or you're crawling in the bush and you decide to crawl left, instead of right, and a mine goes off under the guy who went right. What do you call that, kid?" He ran a hand over the tattoo. "Luck. Fate. War. That's why I'm out here, 'cause I don't want nobody to carry that around inside." Without another word, he moved away, leaving Charlie shaken.

A girl who looked about ten pushed next to Charlie. She was a nubby brown color, with dark, short hair decorated with red barrettes. "Now do me. My name is Akima Lewis and I'm a peace kid. See all my buttons. I have one like yours, too," she announced, pointing to a multitude of political buttons.

"What's a peace kid?" asked Charlie, breathing deeply to help herself relax. The strange man had frightened her so much that she'd forgotten the list of interview questions.

"Peace kids are children like us who stand up for a nuclear-war-free world. We write letters to the Russians telling them what we're like. We march and sing and work for peace," said Akima.

"Why?" Charlie asked.

"Aren't you a peace kid?" Akima asked, her eyes wary.

"Sure, I am," murmured Charlie. "Are you scared?"

"Not as much as I was when I wasn't doing anything," Akima said firmly.

"Want to interview me?" interrupted an Asian man wearing a T-shirt that said STOP NUCLEAR WAR.

"Sure." She watched Akima join a group of children.

By the time Mama Bliss told her they had to leave, they had marched about three miles. Charlie had struggled to complete seven interviews.

Mama Bliss was first to speak in the car. "Cat got your tongue? So what did you think about the march? And Akima?" She swerved around a car, hit the clutch and the brake, then shifted into second gear. "Get some money out of my wallet."

"I never met anybody like Akima. She's so certain about what she believes," said Charlie, handing over a five-dollar bill. The terrifying words of the man with the flat eyes haunted her. She told her grandmother what he had said.

Mama Bliss clucked and shook her head. "Sometimes you find out things you don't want to know."

When Daddy called from Oregon later that day, he sounded far away and exhausted. Charlie was tired, too, and went to bed early, resting her head on the pillow next to Popcorn's. Uncle Ben still wasn't home, and with Sienna spending one more night at Saundra's, peace reigned. Even the animals were behaving. Charlie leaped up. She'd forgotten to call Katie Rose about the march. But deep yawns pushed her back into the soft, warm bed.

On Sunday, after Sienna came home, Mama hauled the family over to visit with Mama Bliss. In the car, Charlie listened to Uncle Ben rave about Dinah. It seemed that

Dinah Sawyer was a travel agent who had her own apartment in San Francisco. She'd never married. Charlie figured she was stuck up and pretty like Sienna.

Still disturbed by the events of the previous day, she headed for the solitude of the dining room, where Mama Bliss kept piles of photo albums scattered around the floor. Over the years, Charlie had avoided those albums that looked ready to fall apart if she touched them. She knew how particular her grandmother was about the photographs. But one album with a torn cover attracted her. Charlie noticed that dozens of photographs had tumbled out over the purple rug and she decided to put them back.

She sat down on the floor. In the kitchen, Granddad was repairing a water faucet and Uncle Ben was taking orders for Chinese food. Mama Bliss was showing Mama her Christmas bottle samples. Sienna was reading a movie magazine.

"Shrimp fried rice for me!" Charlie yelled out.

"Got it!" her uncle called back.

Charlie held up a faded photograph of her grandmother and grandfather at their wedding. They looked so young! Her hands settled on another of her grandfather in an army uniform, standing straight and tall. On the back he'd written, "To my darling, Bliss. All my love, Oscar." Charlie smiled. Her hands reached for a smaller snapshot of a chubby baby with big eyes and two chins—Daddy! And there were more, one when he was learning to walk on bowed legs. She'd never seen these old pictures!

Eagerly, Charlie reached for a pile of smaller photos toppling over her legs. Just above the disarray, a folded newspaper article floated out. Charlie held it up and saw a photograph of a young Black soldier holding another Black soldier in his lap, much like a mother comforting her injured child. One hand reached over to touch another man. It was a white soldier, sprawled on the ground, his eyes open. She stared back at the Black soldier touching him. The recognition hit Charlie with the force of a boxer's punch. That soldier, the one holding his friend, with his hand outstretched, the one with his face turned up to the sky, the one sobbing—he was her father!

"That's Daddy," whispered Charlie. "That's Daddy crying. But it can't be. Daddy never cries." She held the article closer. "But he is my daddy."

Quickly Charlie read the article. The men were her father's friends, Fred Hansen and Gerald Moer. She had never heard him mention them. Reading on, she discovered that her father had been decorated a hero for risking his life to save these men and others.

"Why hasn't anyone in the family ever said that Daddy is a real hero?" she whispered.

Back and forth from the photo to the words her eyes flew. Charlie noticed her father's right leg, twisted in an ugly way and bleeding. "So this is how Daddy injured his leg," she said softly. "Oh, no, they both died!"

The photographs of the Vietnam Memorial in the *National Geographic* magazine came to mind. In her head, Charlie saw the tight-knit rows of names carved on the shiny, black granite panels that Aunt Jessie disliked. The names of all who had died or been listed as missing in action were engraved on the wall. This meant that Fred Hansen and Gerald Moer, her father's friends, were there on one of those panels in Washington, D.C.

Thank goodness her father's name was not there. He was hard to live with, but she was glad he wasn't dead. Charlie wiped at the tears in her eyes. The bitter words of the veteran from the peace march returned. Charlie shivered.

At that moment she heard footsteps. Quickly she refolded the article and hid it away in her sweater pocket. When Sienna asked her what she was doing, Charlie said, "Just straightening up."

Charlie scooted over to let Sienna sit down, barely listening as she rambled on about Joshua Morgan. Mama Bliss had warned her about finding out things she'd rather not know. On her lap a chubby, happy baby boy splashed in the water, while in her pocket the child, grown to man and soldier, wept.

Charlie stared at the yellowed photograph and touched the paper in her pocket, wondering why her father's being a Vietnam hero was a secret. Who could she talk to? Mama? Granddad? Mama Bliss? Uncle Ben? Daddy?

Eight

Life in Mrs. Hayamoto's predictable classroom had its advantages, especially after such a tumultuous weekend. Charlie had spent the rest of Sunday avoiding the family. She'd seized every opportunity to sneak off and stare at the picture of her father and his friends and wonder what it meant.

But this Monday morning those feelings were on hold. Her classmates chattered. The ivy plant drooped. The janitor had forgotten to empty the wastebaskets. As usual, Mr. Rocker stepped in to deliver his "Obey My School Discipline Code" speech. Right in the middle, someone interrupted with an announcement over the intercom about new rainy-day procedures. Mrs. Hayamoto wore her regular Monday morning expression that said, "Why isn't it Friday afternoon?" And Chris Saunders flipped through his three-foot-high stack of clippings and charts, tossing superior looks around like confetti. Only Katie Rose's fumbling and fussing because she'd left something important at one of her parents' was missing.

Charlie decided to annoy Chris. "I went to a peace

march at the university on Saturday, Chris. I got lots of data for my report."

"Good for you," he said. "We're supposed to meet today."

Just then Katie Rose collapsed in her seat. "How about during lunch?" she asked. "Charlie, I heard what you said about the march. I didn't get to go, after all. Mother and Dad had a phone fight, and she got a headache and groaned in bed all day. I spent Sunday at a show to get away from her."

"Why didn't you call me?" asked Charlie.

"Everything jams up inside when they fight, and I can't think straight."

"Divorce is a terrible thing for a kid to go through," added Chris.

Charlie's mouth flew open.

"You can say that again, Chris. Anyway, I did get some books and pamphlets from my brother, so I can share that." Katie Rose started searching. "Let me make sure. I know I brought them. They must be here!"

"I taped seven whole interviews! And that included three kids our age." Charlie grinned, proud of her progress.

"But last week you told me that you had completed a minimum of six interviews." Chris pointed the mechanical pencil at her.

"I lied, Chris. But now I can honestly say that seven are done. I'll talk to my grandfather today and line up some kids here at Hayden. Okay?" Charlie met his stare straight on.

"Sure, Charlie."

That afternoon, after closing time at the store, Charlie trailed Granddad upstairs to his apartment. Four times she started to show him the newspaper article. Then she took the plunge.

"Granddad, do you know anything about Daddy being in Vietnam?"

"What do you want to know, Charlie?" They sat on the gray living room sofa, the recorder between them.

"Is that where he hurt his leg?"

"Yes. Shrapnel wounds. Fragments from a land mine got him."

"Did Daddy do anything special over there?"

"What do you mean by special? My son served two tours of duty as an infantryman in the Twenty-fifth Infantry Division. He fought, got wounded, and came home. Thank God he made it back," said Granddad.

"From what I read, a lot of soldiers died over there." Charlie hoped that her grandfather would speak about Fred Hansen and Gerald Moer. Surely he knew about their dying. Surely he had seen the newspaper clipping. But he simply held his long, thin hands together on his lap and waited. She tried another approach. "I read the magazine you gave me. Thanks, Granddad."

"What did you think of the bronze statue in the article?" he asked.

"The Black soldier reminded me of Daddy," she said. "Do you think Daddy gets sad because of what happened to him in Vietnam?"

He was quiet. "How would you feel coming home in uniform on crutches and being called a 'babykiller'? Some young white girl had the nerve to spit on my son at the airport. She carried a peace sign." He clasped his hands.

"What, Granddad? Somebody spit on Daddy?" Charlie was stunned. It was one thing to read about the Vietnam protest movement of the 1960s and 1970s, when thousands of American college students had marched, burned flags, and battled to stop the war. But to discover that her own father had been spit on was quite another.

"For Black men, going to war means fighting three wars. The war you fight as a soldier. The war you fight there as a Black man. And the war you fight here as a Black man. At least we got parades when we came home from World War II. Even though I had to enter the dining hall by the back door because I was Black, while German prisoners of war sauntered right through the front door." He snorted. "Right here in America."

Charlie realized that Granddad had forgotten her. He was pacing up and down the living room, talking to the ceiling. "My son didn't even get a parade. Not even a thank-you. And there he was, a disabled Vietnam veteran with no job. A part of him just folded into himself. Who can blame him?"

The question hit Charlie. Mama had been so right. There was so much she didn't know about her own father.

Suddenly Granddad shook his head furiously from side to side, as if emptying loose debris. He stopped before her, his proud eyes wide and clear. "Did I ever answer your question?"

"Sure, Granddad," she said. This interview was over. Now she understood why Daddy hated her project. But how could she quit?

On Tuesday night Charlie finally heard her father come

home. From the bedroom, she listened to Sienna's welcome, as well as her mother's. There were happy cries, and the rare sound of his deep laugh flowed all the way down the hall to her. Then the bedroom door opened.

"Your mother told me about how good you were at school while I was in Oregon," he said, standing by her bed. She eased away a few inches. "That makes me happy, Charlie."

Charlie gazed up. Daddy's face looked nothing like the one in the newspaper article and barely resembled the angry one that she had last seen. No, tonight his eyes shone and his smile was for her, too.

"Hi, Daddy. Welcome home," she said.

"You all right? Got a cold or something?" he asked anxiously, and reached to touch her forehead.

"No, I'm fine," Charlie said.

"Feels like I've been away from my family for months. I hate the traveling and paperwork, but if I want the job, I have to go." He sighed and sat down on the bed. "Your mother says you've really been a help to her."

Charlie felt shaky. He did look like the Black soldier in the bronze statue that was part of the Vietnam Memorial in Washington, D.C. She wished she could go there and see for herself. She looked at her father's muscular chest and neck and his large head. She could count the thick black hairs in his mustache. Daddy. Impulsively, she reached up and placed a quick, light kiss on his cheek.

"What did I do to deserve that?" he said, a flush darkening his cheeks.

"I missed you."

"I'll have to stay away more often. I've been a little

rough on you, Charlie. Did some thinking while I was gone. If you believe I hate you, then somehow I've failed." He cleared his throat. "Sienna and I are going to get ice cream. Want to come, too?"

"Daddy?"

"Yes?" He stood up and waited.

"If I asked to interview you for my social studies report, how mad would you get at me?" Charlie held her breath.

"I knew this was coming. I can't talk to you about that project. Not now. Not ever." He stood in the doorway like a sentry. "You want to come with us for ice cream?"

"Sure, Daddy," Charlie said, disappointed but relieved, because at least she had mustered the grit to ask him. "There's something else. It doesn't have anything to do with Vietnam. Mama told me a story about when you were a little boy and some stray dogs. Did you win?"

He threw back his head and laughed. "So Ellie's been telling my old secrets! She never forgets anything. No, Charlie, I lost, but I sure gave them a good fight. I'm going to change. Then we'll go."

Charlie let herself be swept into the family celebration. When Uncle Ben came home, her father's exuberance extended to him as well. They spent the evening laughing around the kitchen table, eating cartons of ice cream and the rest of the candy.

During that night and the days that followed, Charlie watched her father furtively for some sign of the hero in the newspaper article. One evening she thought about showing him the photo, but stopped. She didn't want to start any trouble.

Mama and Daddy were listening to jazz in the family

room, snuggled close. Uncle Ben was out with the mysterious Dinah. Sienna had taken to her room, writing letters that she hid away. Her sister and uncle lived in worlds of their own.

By the first week in October, orange and black streamers and skeletons decorated Berkeley store windows. Since the peace march, Charlie had completed four interviews at school: two with first-graders, one with a second-grader, and one with a third-grader. With the additional practice, her questions improved. She was learning to listen.

At the same time, Charlie was learning to see better, too. But even if she'd been oblivious, she would have noticed that Sienna had been coming home late for over a week. She didn't even run with Daddy anymore. What was going on?

Finally, during recess and lunch one day, the last student interviews were scheduled. There was an enclave in the schoolyard created by the joining of the old Hayden school building and the new one-story addition. Bordered on three sides by the tan structures, the center boasted a fine Douglas fir tree with a circular wooden bench around the trunk. Here Charlie set up her office. On a lower branch of the tree she hung a sign, CHARLIE PIPPIN, INTERVIEWER, painted in black on a red background.

Three girls jumped double-dutch. They shouted chants to the sounds of the ropes hitting the concrete. Groups of children played. Katie Rose sat next to Charlie, her beret pulled to the right side.

"Got to put my official outfit on," said Charlie, taking the jewelry, sunglasses, and Vietnam buttons out of the briefcase.

"You look ready," teased Katie Rose.

"You're looking better," retorted Charlie. "The clothes match today."

"I sat down with my parents last night and told them that this going back and forth was too hard on me." Katie Rose twisted a strand of straight brown hair.

"You did! What happened?"

"Mother started to cry. Dad got upset. Then they insisted that I see a therapist. You know what I told them?"

"Nope."

"I actually told them they were the ones who needed a psychiatrist! All I needed was some routine. I couldn't believe I said that." She gave Charlie a wan smile. "Guess hanging around you rubs off."

"I wish it would rub off on me. Come on, I want to finish three today. Let me see. Who's first? Gregory Jenkins!" She yelled out the boy's name.

A tall, skinny Black boy wearing a blue plaid shirt ambled over. "Here I am. Shoot."

"Your name, room, and grade, please," stated Charlie in her official reporter voice.

"Gregory Martin Jenkins, the Great One. Room 207. Grade Five," he replied.

"Tell me what you know about the Vietnam War."

At the end of the interview, Charlie asked Gregory to share three wishes with her. The clowning around stopped. Staring up at the dark green branches, he said, "No war. No nuclear war. Peace on earth."

During the last interview, with a third-grade girl named Sherise Holiday, the clouds darkened. At one point Sherise tugged at Charlie's sleeve. "I just don't understand why countries want to *kill* each other. Charlie, are they going to blow up the world?" The eight-year-old girl's voice quaked. "And kill everybody?"

It wasn't the first time she'd heard those questions. The wind blew in a cold gust, almost taking her hat off. What should she say? Akima would know.

"Maybe not if we speak up," said Katie Rose. "Right, Charlie?"

"I hope so," answered Charlie, glad that Sherise was the last one. This project was getting depressing. Her attempts to interview the few Vietnamese and Laotian students at school had been frustrating. They had wanted to talk about how good life in America was, not about the countries they had left. Charlie had managed to learn that to their families the chance to live in America had been worth risking their lives. Anyway, Charlie had enough material, and there was no need to interview Sienna's friends. That was a blessing.

During the second week in the month, Uncle Ben got a phone call from a former college roommate offering him a job in San Francisco—a good one. To Charlie's astonishment, he informed the family that he was going to take the position, fly back to Chicago, pack up, and move to California.

Uncle Ben invited Charlie to walk around the block. He had an hour before he had to leave for the airport. Next door, in the Neilsons' front window, a jagged-toothed jack-o'-lantern leered at her. She stuck her tongue out.

"You'll come back soon?" she asked, more out of curiosity than need.

Uncle Ben handed her a stick of bubble gum. "In about

two weeks. I promise I'll be back in time to take you trick-or-treating for Halloween! You know, we never got to talk about your report."

"Yeah, I know."

"I feel bad about that, Charlie. But I'll find a way to make this up to you."

"Okay, Uncle Ben." Charlie decided to let it go. "I finished, anyway."

"What did you find out?" he asked.

"Most of the kids are scared they won't grow up because a nuclear war is going to destroy everything. Most of them don't know much about Vietnam. But they know that they want peace." She paused. "About all of them said we should get rid of the nuclear bombs, missiles, and guns."

"Did you get to talk to your grandfather or father?"

"Just Granddad. Daddy didn't want to."

"I can understand that. Like most families, we keep our secrets." He blew a pink bubble, then popped it.

"Why?"

"Because we're afraid to hurt each other."

"Uncle Ben, did you ever visit the Vietnam Memorial in Washington, D.C.?"

He was silent. "No . . . I've put off taking care of that piece of business."

Charlie was only partially listening to his answer because she was thinking about her father.

"I found something, Uncle Ben, but you can't tell Daddy. Promise?" Charlie handed him the newspaper article.

He sat down on a bench at a bus stop. "Where in the world did you find this?"

"In one of Mama Bliss's old albums."

"No wonder Oscar never talked about his last tour in Vietnam. He had a rough war," he murmured.

Charlie touched his left hand. "Why did you and Daddy go if it was so horrible?"

He stood up, his face tired, and looked out at the traffic. "We believed in our country. Black men have fought for this country in every single war. And Black women, too."

"Why is Daddy being a hero such a secret, Uncle Ben?"

"Because remembering something like this hurts, Charlie. It hurts bad. I don't think the family is keeping some big secret. But no one wants to upset your father. Since he doesn't talk about this, who can?"

He handed her the article. "I've got a plane to catch. You'd better put this back where it belongs."

On Tuesday of the next week, Sienna got caught. Daddy had come home early. Charlie walked in near the end of the argument, amazed to hear her father yelling at her sister.

"I want the truth, Sienna! Where have you been?" he demanded. "Do you think I'm blind?"

"I was in the library, working on my English term paper, Daddy." Sienna's face was red and hot.

"I don't believe you!"

Then the phone rang, and Charlie grabbed it. She recognized the voice immediately. Joshua Morgan, basketball star. Charlie pretended that she was speaking with someone else. When she hung up, she knew why Sienna was coming home late.

Later, Sienna pushed Charlie into their bedroom and shut the door. "You know where I've been, don't you?"

Charlie nodded. "You've been with Joshua. Joshua Morgan."

"All we do is talk, Charlie. I'll pay you three dollars if you don't tell Daddy. No, five." Sienna reached for her wallet. "You know Daddy won't let me have company for another year. Please, Charlie, help me." Sienna looked desperate.

Charlie weighed her options. She'd never tell on Sienna, anyway. That would be snitching, and she was no snitch! On the other hand, if Sienna was willing to offer her money, she'd be silly not to take it. "Okay, I'll cover for you, but I don't like lying to Daddy and Mama. I really don't, Sienna." Charlie held out her hand. Sienna gave her the money. She placed the five dollars in her sweater pocket, next to the newspaper article.

The war and peace committee met at Charlie's house after school the next afternoon. Charlie had made arrangements with her grandfather not to help him in the store. While Katie Rose and Chris set out their notebooks on the dining room table, Charlie yanked cheeses, pickles, potato chips, and bread out of the refrigerator, throwing the food onto two platters.

While she was still in the kitchen, the telephone rang. "Hi, Pippin residence," she said.

"Rebel, just wanted to check and see if anybody was home. I promised your mother I'd drop off some of my bottles for her to sell at the hospital. I'll be by later on."

Before Charlie could tell her that she was in the middle of an important committee meeting, her grandmother was gone.

"Now all I need is for Sienna to come sneaking in here

right after Daddy gets home!" she sputtered, plastering a smile on her face as she joined her classmates.

While Chris was reciting his summaries of the dozens of articles he'd collected about war, the telephone rang again. "Excuse me, I'm sorry," Charlie apologized, stumbling out of the chair. "Yes, *who* is it?"

"Charlie! Is your mother home yet?" It was Uncle Ben.

"Nope, and Daddy told me this morning he'd be late. How's Chicago?"

"Fine. I'll be back in about a week. And I haven't forgotten about Halloween. Give your mother this phone number so she knows where to reach me," he said.

By the time Charlie had returned and Chris had picked up where he'd left off, the doorbell rang.

"You certainly live in a chaotic environment," he said, wrinkling his nose. "How do you manage to study?"

"I'm a genius, so I don't need to study!" Charlie snapped, flinging open the door without asking who was there.

With his arms loaded with groceries and Mama Bliss behind him, her father cursed as some oranges hit the floor and rolled across the throw rugs. He bent down to clutch one of the bags. "What's going on here?" he asked.

"Mama said I could invite them over. We're doing schoolwork," explained Charlie, the rubber band, which had been still so long, snapping again inside her stomach.

"Hello, sir. My name is Christopher Saunders." Chris held out his hand and then, realizing that both of Mr. Pippin's arms were full, withdrew it, laughing self-consciously.

"Hi, Mr. Pippin and Mrs. Pippin." Katie Rose took one

of the bags of tree bottles from Mama Bliss.

"You're early," said Charlie, scurrying toward the kitchen, hoping that he would close his eyes and follow blindly.

He stopped and put down the groceries. "Vietnam. Nuclear war. Peace buttons. Newspaper articles. Graphs. Fliers. Pamphlets. Tape recorder. This is that war and peace project, isn't it?"

"Mr. Pippin, you'd be impressed with what we've learned," piped up Chris. "I am confident that our report is going to be rated as outstanding by Mrs. Hayamoto."

"Why did you have to hold the meeting here, in my house? You know how I feel about these things," Mr. Pippin said to Charlie.

"I thought you'd be home late, and this was the only place we had to meet."

"Oh, Oscar, does it matter? The child is here doing her work! Come on, get your coat off. You're looking like a bear with a bee on its nose. Charlie, finish up. Oscar, I need your help with these bags," said Mama Bliss, moving down the hall like a freight train.

"We'll finish this later!" Without another word, he headed for the kitchen, leaving a red-faced Charlie behind.

In low tones, Chris finished sharing the facts he'd collected. "Too many wars for me!" he concluded. "What did you find out, Katie Rose?"

"You know my brother goes to UC–Berkeley? Well, he gave me a lot of information about nuclear war. The more I read, the more frightened I got," she said, quickly passing around the pamphlets. "But there are organizations that are trying to stop the proliferation of nuclear capability.

Hear my fancy language?" She smiled. "That just means that groups of grown-ups, including doctors, and kids like us are trying to stop the production of more nuclear weapons."

At that moment Sienna, a quiet question in her eyes, walked past, acknowledging Charlie's nod that told her their father was home. And shortly afterward Mr. Pippin headed out to jog, Sienna right behind him. Then Mama Bliss left, wishing the committee good luck.

After discussing Charlie's interviews, the group decided on the order of presentation. They rehearsed for about half an hour and agreed to meet again, at school.

Charlie stood up. "I've been thinking that we want to make our report different from the other groups'. I mean, we have so many scary, unbelievable, life-and-death, downright depressing facts to present."

"Well? Come on, Charlie, I'm due home in exactly ten minutes," Chris said, zipping up his green jacket.

"Charlie, I'm not doing anything crazy," teased Katie Rose.

"You know that girl I told you about, Akima? I've been thinking about her saying she was a 'peace kid,' and I thought we could combine Halloween and our report."

"Charlie, what are you talking about?"

"Chris, just listen. What about painting our faces with peace symbols? I know how to do it, and we'd look unique. Rainbows, trees, flowers, stars, hearts, hands joined together."

The room got quiet. Katie Rose and Chris frowned at Charlie.

"It might lighten the tone. Sure would get Mrs.

Hayamoto's attention. Right, Chris?" offered Katie Rose.

"Is there anything in Mr. Rocker's Discipline Code about painting your face? I refuse to jeopardize the high probability that I will be one of the thirty to go to Disneyland."

"I checked the Code and there's nothing against it."

"Frankly, Charlie, the idea of rainbows and flowers on my face is ludicrous." He shook his head.

"Would bombs and blood fit your image?"

"You've got a point, Charlie. Let's decide at our next meeting," suggested Katie Rose.

The next Monday, the committee met at school. After an intense discussion, a compromise was reached. Charlie would paint her face. Katie Rose would wear her buttons and carry a sign. And Chris would wear his three-piece navy blue suit, white shirt, and red tie. They were finally ready for the big day.

Nine

Tuesday morning, the war and peace committee gathered. They had decided that Chris should go first, then Katie Rose, and, last of all, Charlie. The girls helped Chris tape the large world map to the front of the room and rest his charts and graphs on the blackboard ledge. Charlie suppressed a smile when he set up a small wooden podium and picked up a pointer.

"I'd like to begin," Chris said, "by acknowledging the help I've received from librarians in Berkeley and the other members of the war and peace committee. When I first began the challenge of assessing the number and kinds of wars being fought around the world, I felt quite confident that gathering the data would be easy." He paused and frowned. "That *was* the easy part. The hard part was trying to accept what I learned."

Charlie leaned forward, listening as Chris pointed to the areas on the map marked with red paper guns. According to magazine articles he'd read, in 1983 there were forty-five nations at war—one-fourth of the countries in the world. Charlie noticed several red guns in Asia, the

Mideast, and Africa, as well as in Latin America and Europe.

"Looks like everyone is at war except us," Katie Rose whispered to Charlie. This was the first time Chris had unveiled the map.

"Not exactly," said Charlie, "but close."

At this point Chris was saying that since the end of World War II in 1945, there had been approximately one hundred and twenty-five wars fought.

"That's in less than fifty years!" exclaimed Mrs. Hayamoto.

Chris nodded in solemn agreement. "Of course the 1983 count is not entirely accurate for 1985. More wars and guerrilla movements have to be added. Several appear to be backed by Russian and Cuban weapons, money, military advisors and some troops. The United States is also involved. We still have thousands of American troops in South Korea to keep communist North Korea from crossing over. And we supply Israel with military aid. And don't forget our military presence and money in countries like Nicaragua and El Salvador."

Chris continued, describing specific wars and listing bleak statistics of the dead and wounded.

Mrs. Hayamoto waited until he was through. "Christopher, what did you learn from your report?"

Charlie grimaced at Katie Rose. They hadn't expected that question.

Chris Saunders loosened his tie, put down the pointer, and stepped from behind the podium. "There's fighting going on in Vietnam and Kampuchea, Israel and Lebanon, Nicaragua, El Salvador, Iran and Iraq, Ethiopia, a French

Pacific island called New Caledonia, Northern Ireland, Afghanistan, and more places I'm too tired to name. Right now, this is happening! And a lot of these conflicts have been going on for years. I learned that people are not naturally peaceful. Living in peace must take more intelligence than most people use. Knowing that makes me feel depressed."

Mrs. Hayamoto smiled and shook her head. "Then you have learned a great deal. Now you can give some thought to what you can do to improve this sad state of affairs."

The class clapped as Chris gathered his materials and sat down.

While everyone took a recess break, Charlie and Chris helped Katie Rose set up. "How did I do?" Chris asked.

Katie Rose was arranging a stack of pamphlets put out by an anti-nuclear war group called Physicians for Social Responsibility, while Charlie leaned her sign against the back wall. "Great, Chris," said Katie Rose. "You got the report off to a terrific start. I just hope I can get through this."

Charlie stared over at him, not sure of what to say. Chris had taught her something important, that someone as unemotional as he seemed could be touched and affected by their report. For the first time she suspected that his way of talking and acting disguised a real kid.

"Charlie? What is your opinion?" he asked.

"You held up your end, Chris," she teased.

He grinned.

When the class had gathered, Katie Rose picked up the NO NUKES sign and marched to the front of the room. She began with a map, too, a map of the city of Berkeley, with

Hayden Elementary School and the downtown area circled. In slow, measured tones, she described what would happen if a single, one-megaton nuclear bomb was dropped on Berkeley, California.

"A one-megaton nuclear bomb equals one million tons of dynamite. There are more than fifty thousand nuclear weapons in the world. The United States has about thirty thousand, and Russia has about twenty thousand. We know that France, England, and China have some, too. So, understand, I am just talking about one, one-megaton bomb. Some nuclear bombs are twenty megatons!" she said, stopping to catch her breath.

Charlie noticed that the class was silent in a strange way. It was as if no one dared to breathe. She had heard this information before, but the facts were scary enough to raise goose bumps on her arms.

"Every person, every single child, all of us would be immediately killed. This is the downtown area. Here's Berkeley High School. Everything in this area would vanish in a hole twenty stories deep. Let's say you were on the Bay Bridge or farther away in the cities of Richmond, Alameda, or Moraga. You would have a fifty-fifty chance of being killed right away or getting third-degree burns all over your body." She stopped. "What's horrible is that there wouldn't be any medical help. Those poor people who weren't killed outright would suffer awful burns, blindness, ruptured eardrums, and radiation poisoning."

"I don't want to hear any more," yelled a girl from the back.

"Neither did I!" retorted Katie Rose. "But my brother told me that the only way I could get over feeling so scared was to learn and do something. So listen."

Charlie and Chris grinned at each other. Katie Rose was showing spunk.

"What makes this terrible is that I read that by the year 2000, thirty-four more countries will have nuclear bombs. And with all those wars Chris told us about, there's a big chance somebody will use a nuclear bomb and start a war. Some people say that if that happened, over half of the world's population, about two billion people, would die soon. The rest would die in the dark, cold months after."

Finally, Katie Rose reached the end of her report. She explained how important it was for kids to be active. On a chart she had listed steps to take. They included talking with family, friends, and teachers, joining groups that worked for peace, donating money to peace groups, studying more about peace in school, and even demonstrating.

"Last year I went with my brother on a demonstration to protest the work a laboratory near here is doing to make nuclear weapons. That was my first demonstration. For the first time I didn't feel so alone. I felt united and strong. So don't sit around being scared. Do something!" she urged.

Mrs. Hayamoto started the applause. "Well, we know what you learned from your report, Kathryn Rose! Thank you for the pamphlets. I hope everyone will take them home. Let's take a stretch, and then we'll hear from Chartreuse."

"I thought I was going to faint, Charlie," Katie Rose said, dropping into her seat.

"But you did great!" her two committee members said in unison.

"That's the first and last oral report I intend to give in sixth grade." She smiled. "Charlie, we'll help you get ready. You've got to give your report and pull everything together so that the class understands what our committee is about."

Charlie wrinkled her nose. "Thanks for making me feel so relaxed, Katie Rose."

The green and yellow flowers on her cheeks sparkled under the fluorescent lights. Dots of gold glittered on Charlie's face. She had taped her map of Vietnam to the blackboard. She turned to it and began her speech. "From Chris, you learned about the wars around the world. And from Katie Rose you learned about nuclear warfare and ways to work for peace. I am the last member of our committee to report. Why? Because I wanted to tell you about one war, the one that my father fought and was hurt in. How many of your relatives fought in Vietnam?" she asked, watching at least a dozen hands go up, including Mrs. Hayamoto's. "Vietnam was the longest war this country ever fought and the only one we lost. Some books say the war started in 1950, when President Truman sent thirty-five American military advisors to help the French fight in Vietnam. Others use the year 1965, when the first United States Marine battalion landed in Da Nang. The war ended in 1975, when the communists took over South Vietnam. Look at the map so you know where Vietnam is. That's where our relatives went to fight when they were only eighteen or nineteen years old.

"You should know that over two and one half million Americans, men and women, went to Vietnam. Over fifty-four thousand were killed and over three hundred thousand wounded. My father and my uncle were wounded. So this war is part of my life.

"One book I read said that the United States spent more than one hundred billion dollars fighting the Vietnam War. Think about how many hungry people that money could feed, how many sick babies could be helped." She paused. "And our teachers are always saying that they don't get paid enough! Just a little bit of that money could have gone to Mrs. Hayamoto!"

The teacher smiled. "I'll vote for that, Chartreuse." The class laughed.

"The South Vietnamese lost more than two hundred thousand soldiers and had approximately half a million wounded. It was hard to judge how many of the communist North Vietnamese were killed or injured because after a fight they dragged away as many of the bodies as they could. The estimates go as high as a million killed and three million wounded."

"Everybody lost," a boy in the front muttered.

"You better believe it," Charlie said.

After sharing how scared and uncertain the kids she'd interviewed felt, Charlie added, "Katie Rose was right when she said that taking action makes you feel better. In a peace march I met a girl named Akima who isn't afraid. Neither is my grandmother. She demonstrates, and she doesn't care what anybody thinks about her. And Chris was right when he said that intelligent people seek peace. I hope we can be that kind of people."

The applause rang out as the three children stood together in front of the room. They grinned at one another, proud of their hard work. Charlie looked at Katie Rose and especially Chris. She had learned more about war and peace from them. And they had learned from her. There was something to be said for teamwork.

"War and peace committee, you've done an outstanding job," said Mrs. Hayamoto, clapping hard. "I'm very proud of you."

On the way back to the classroom, after scrubbing her face, Charlie felt in her pocket. That morning she'd made sure to bring the newspaper article for good luck. Over the weeks of rereading it and staring at the photograph, she had grown closer to her father's friends, Gerald Moer and Fred Hansen. Burying them back in the old album had felt wrong. But what was the right thing to do?

Ten

The next day Charlie started a serious search for a place to paint Halloween faces. Earlier, Granddad had refused to let her set up a card table in front of the store. So Charlie scouted the school, ruling out the playgrounds. During lunch with Katie Rose, she leaped up and ran out down the long basement hallway, took a right, then a left. Tucked there, far from Mr. Rocker's beaten path, was the oldest, shabbiest room at Hayden—the unused bookroom. The door was open, so Charlie peeked in. Dust covered the sagging bookshelves, stacks of discarded textbooks, and the faded linoleum floor. The room was also windowless. There were no light bulbs in the fixtures. Charlie realized that she'd need some sort of light. Luckily a table and some folding chairs stood in one corner. She grinned in the darkness. Charlie Pippin was back in business! One challenge remained.

Back at the lunch table, Charlie told Katie Rose about her plan to use a special advertising campaign in which they would whisper the date, place, and cost of the face painting. That way Mr. Rocker couldn't find out.

Katie Rose was back in her disheveled state. "But I can't get into trouble, Charlie. My parents would die! Mother's close to a nervous breakdown," she moaned.

"This is foolproof. We'll only tell the customers I know. They can keep their mouths shut. Come on, don't back out on me. We're a team, right?" Charlie urged. "I need a partner, Katie Rose."

"I'm scared!"

"Do you want to be afraid all of your life? You'll get part of the profits and see how exciting being in business is."

Brushing back her hair, Katie Rose smiled. "I am curious, Charlie. You're sure we won't get caught, because I'm telling you the truth, I can't get into any trouble right now!"

Charlie grinned. "Don't worry. I've got it all figured out." They shook hands across the lunchroom table.

When Uncle Ben returned from Chicago two days before Halloween, true to his word, Charlie was surprised.

Mr. Pippin looked up from the magazine he was reading in front of the fireplace. Earlier, after a run with Sienna, he'd fixed a pot of jambalaya, a delicious mixture of rice, shrimp, chicken, sausage, Creole spices, and tomatoes. Charlie was setting the table for five, hoping that Uncle Ben would stay for dinner and give her a chance to ask him for help. With the face-painting supplies, she and Katie Rose would need a ride to school early Halloween morning.

"Ben, how did Chicago go?" her father asked, his normally gruff voice less hostile.

"Great. I made arrangements to have my furniture shipped here and put in storage until I get a place to stay," said Uncle Ben.

"From what I've been hearing, there might be a wedding soon."

Charlie moved out of her father's view so she could still see him without being seen. She was startled when her uncle sank down on the sofa.

"I don't know, Oscar. Dinah seems to think I need to take care of some unfinished business before I can 'make a commitment.'" He emphasized the last words. "Why are women so hard to understand?"

Charlie waited for her father's reply.

He fell out laughing! "Ben, don't ask me! I live with three of them! I've got Eleanor telling me to go easy on Charlie! Charlie running around like one of those sixties hippies who got out of going to war any way they could. By the way, where is she?" He stared around. "Charlie!"

Charlie froze, not daring to breathe.

"Guess she's in the kitchen. In my own house, I've got a peace nut! You know what I mean?"

"Yeah," Uncle Ben said, laughing. When did the two of them start agreeing? Charlie wondered.

"Dinah told me that females are the superior species, Oscar." Uncle Ben chuckled.

"I've got Sienna acting like she's grown! What in the world happened to my beautiful little girl? Lying to me and Ellie about where's she been!" He held his head like it hurt. "And my mother, demonstrating, painting bottles when she ought to be taking care of my dad! What does my dad do? He goes on his way, seeing Mama, running the store."

102

"Sometimes it's hard to understand the people we love. Look, as soon as I can get a place, I'll be moving, Oscar," said Ben, rising. "I don't want to take advantage of your and Ellie's hospitality. With this new job, it's time I got on with my life."

"Yeah. Okay, Ben. Sorry about running off at the mouth like that." Her father laughed in an embarrassed way. "Guess I got carried away."

Charlie eased back into the hallway, bumping into her mother. She excused herself and went to the bedroom, where Sienna was busily writing another letter.

"Who's that to?" Charlie asked.

Sienna paused long enough to reach down and stroke Sheba's silky fur. "I've got a pen pal in Peru."

"Sienna, do you think I'm a peace nut?"

"You mean one of those fanatics who lets herself get dragged to jail?" she asked, finally twisting to face Charlie. "Yeah."

"Nope. But for some weird reason, you're interested in learning about the Vietnam War. And after interviewing all those people, look what you found out. Everybody is scared. I could have told you that and saved you time, tape, and trouble."

Charlie eyed her older sister. Sienna was still dressed in her gray jogging suit. "Do you worry?"

"Only when I decide to waste my time. But why should I, Charlie? There are better things to do." She snorted. "And what can anybody *do* to stop a nuclear war or another Vietnam? Nothing."

"I don't believe that, Sienna," shouted Charlie.

"Neither do I." Mrs. Pippin frowned at them from the doorway. "Sienna, sometimes I am ashamed of you! Do you know that less than forty years ago, your daddy and I, your family, couldn't eat, sleep, vote, or shop wherever we wanted to? What made that change? People protesting, that's what. People have changed history."

"All right, Mama, don't get upset. I've got homework to do," said Sienna, turning away. Charlie waited to see what her mother would do.

"Oh, no, Miss Sienna! You're not turning me off like a water faucet!" said Mrs. Pippin, marching into the room.

"Mama, do you believe that my project was wrong?" interrupted Charlie.

"No. Just try to understand how your father sees things, Charlie."

Now Sienna spoke up. "I didn't mean to make you ashamed of me, Mama. It's just that all of that civil rights stuff happened a long time ago. It's over. Everyone's equal now."

"If you believe that, Sienna, you've got a lot to learn," warned Mrs. Pippin. "And learn the hardest way, with life kicking you in the rear! Get up and help me get Sunday dinner on the table."

Halloween morning dawned cold and foggy. Katie Rose had spent the night with Charlie, sleeping at the other end of the bed, her feet tucked against Popcorn's soft coat. The girls were up early. Daddy had gone back to Oregon yesterday, and Mama was still asleep, enjoying a vacation day, which meant they just had to sneak past Sienna, and that was a snap.

Best of all, Uncle Ben had stayed for dinner and had agreed to drive them to school on his way to San Francisco.

As soon as the girls had set up shop, the customers began to arrive, sneaking into the bookroom. Charlie and Katie Rose worked together, painting faces, counting change, and keeping an eye on the doorway.

Most girls asked for a white face, red mouth, eye color, and a few pink and glitter hearts on their cheeks. But the boys insisted on horrible monster faces. Black triangles around the nostrils, red and black fangs below the bottom lip, and black and red paint dripping from the eyes. Monster faces took longer. But with help from Katie Rose, Charlie finished. They promised the kids to be there after school.

By the time they had packed up, the late buzzer rang. Rushing, Charlie stowed the supplies in a dark corner. But several children arrived late, so Mrs. Hayamoto didn't notice.

The annual school Halloween parade was held during the morning recess. Charlie marched around the neighborhood with the rest of her class. She was dressed as a businesswoman in an old suit of her mother's, high heels, a brown cloche hat, and her briefcase. And she was wearing the Vietnam buttons.

Neighbors waved from the houses and apartment windows. Draculas, spiders, skeletons, witches, werewolves, and leopards marched along. Mr. Rocker was dressed in a graduation cap and gown. And Mrs. Hayamoto wore a football uniform, complete with shoulder pads and helmet! One of the second-graders, who was in a wheelchair, waved at Charlie and pointed happily at her face, which Charlie had painted. That made her feel great!

During the Halloween party, while Charlie munched on a cupcake, Mrs. Hayamoto said she had an important announcement to make. There was going to be a District Oratory Contest. The social studies projects had been a step to prepare them for the contest. Chris Saunders nudged Charlie. The winner of the room contest would go on to represent their sixth-grade classroom in the school competition. That winner would compete against sixth-grade winners from two other schools in Berkeley. Mrs. Hayamoto told them to start writing their speeches and rehearsing, and she nodded firmly at Charlie.

But Charlie had business on her mind. After school, she and Katie Rose skulked down to the basement. While she was sprinkling silver glitter on a star, Charlie suddenly thought about getting caught.

"You know what, Charlie? Being in business is great!" Katie Rose whispered.

"As long as you don't get caught," Charlie reminded her. "Hold the flashlight steady."

"How can we?" Katie Rose asked.

While Charlie finished the last girl, Katie Rose took a bathroom break. Charlie looked up. For a second she thought she saw somebody pass the doorway and pause, but she couldn't be certain. When her friend returned, Charlie threw their things into the shopping bags and pushed Katie Rose out of there as fast as she could, hoping she hadn't left anything behind in the dim room.

That afternoon Charlie enjoyed the traditional, messy carving of the pumpkin and baking of the pumpkin seeds. During the dark, cloudless night, she, Katie Rose, and Uncle Ben walked from one house to another, trick-or-treating. People had placed lighted candles inside their carved pumpkins and lined them on the front steps of their houses, creating an eerie, sinister sight.

The wind was high. Small groups of children dashed past them, running up steps, knocking on doors, stuffing pillow cases, bags, and plastic pumpkins with treats. Obeying her father's rule, Charlie and Katie Rose waited to open their candy. Better to be safe than sorry, as Mama Bliss would say.

The best part of Halloween was dumping all the candy on her bed, then counting and inventorying each piece. "I got fifteen percent more than last year, Sienna," Charlie announced. But her sister was too busy writing another letter to Joshua. Ignoring her, the girls concentrated on their loot. When Katie Rose brought up the oratory contest, Charlie shushed her. It was wonderful to push aside school and Vietnam. "I don't want to think about anything right now except all of this great candy!" she said. And then, in a low tone, "And all the money we made today!"

The summons to the principal's office had come the next morning after recess. A pained expression crossed Mr. Rocker's face. In his hand he held the flashlight and two tubes of face paint.

For a while, Charlie hoped she'd escape with a reprimand. So she was shaken when Mr. Rocker telephoned Mama to come to the school. The principal was considering suspending her! Daddy was due home that evening. The last thing Charlie wanted was for him to discover that she was in trouble. Again.

Before school ended, Charlie trudged down the long, dim hallway to the principal's office. This time her mother, Granddad, and Mama Bliss were there. During a hasty conference outside, they told her that they didn't approve of the way she'd handled the Halloween face painting business, but they felt that suspension was too harsh.

Mr. Rocker hadn't expected the Pippin family to show up. He called to his secretary for more chairs. In terse sentences he laid out the case against Charlie, citing the face painting, the tardies in September, the pencil enterprise, and the origami business. He refused to name the person who had reported Charlie, saying only that the person was an instructional aide on his team. Just then, Mrs. Hayamoto came in and sat down next to Mama. Charlie leaned close to Granddad, wondering what was going to happen to her.

Mama Bliss lit the fireworks. "As far as I'm concerned, this entire meeting takes the rag off the bush! How could you think about suspending a child for showing a little American initiative and creativity?" she demanded.

"Excuse me, Mrs. Pippin, I didn't catch that. 'Takes the rag off the bush'?" asked Mr. Rocker, adjusting his tie, a bright yellow with green clover leaves.

"A plain folks' saying, Mr. Rocker. Means that a person is flabbergasted, amazed, astonished, stunned, shocked, surprised, taken aback! Does that clear things up for you?" Mama Bliss leaned forward. Charlie knew that in three seconds her grandmother would jump up and start a speech about America being a free country where human beings have certain "inalienable rights."

But Mrs. Hayamoto spoke up before she could. "Mr. Rocker, I have to say that over the past several weeks there has been a considerable improvement in Chartreuse's attitude. She comes to class on time and works hard, and she's earned more points for following the Discipline Code. Also, her social studies project was excellent." Mrs. Hayamoto paused. "I do think Chartreuse's 'creative activities' should cease. But detention might be better than suspension."

Mama and Granddad nodded. Charlie kept her eye on Mr. Rocker. With a scowl he asked the one question she feared. "Where is Mr. Pippin?"

"My husband is out of town on business, Mr. Rocker. I believe that you can count on me to discipline my daughter." Mrs. Pippin stared the principal right in the eye.

"The school Discipline Code is supposed to encourage learning, right? Charlie needs to be here to learn, don't you agree?" Granddad asked quietly.

When Charlie walked out of the office, flanked by her family, she let out a deep breath. Detention Hall until Christmas break! But she knew that the victory was lasting only as long as her father didn't find out. In the car, she promised her mother to stop being a businesswoman. "There's no room for my kind of creativity at Hayden."

When Charlie and her mother reached home, after stopping at the cleaners and grocery store, they heard the sounds of Daddy arguing with Uncle Ben. Charlie cringed. They found Uncle Ben sitting across from Daddy at the dining table. Mr. Rocker's secretary had called just after Daddy had gotten home to tell Charlie that detention would start on Tuesday, not Monday, because of a faculty meeting. Sienna had given the telephone to Daddy. From the expression on her father's face and the guilty nod from her uncle, Charlie realized that Daddy knew everything.

"All right, what's going on in this family? My own

mother lends you her supplies! And you, Ben, you drive Charlie to school!" He threw up his hands. "You were wrong to help Charlie. This is my family."

"You're right, Oscar," Uncle Ben said. "I think it's time for me to start that new life. You've been more than good to me. Ellie, I'll call later. Sorry."

"Oh, Ben, please don't go," Mama said.

And Charlie's father added, "Ben, you know you don't have to go."

"It's time," Ben said.

Miserable, Charlie watched her uncle leave the room to pack. In less than twenty minutes, he gave her a kiss and walked out the door. Charlie heard the camper's engine start up.

The living room was still and silent. Charlie's father wouldn't even look at her. When her mother nodded, she got up and went to her room to find her sister in tears.

"Why did you give the phone to Daddy, Sienna?" she demanded.

"I didn't know what the school was calling about. She asked for you, then Mama. You all weren't home. Don't blame me for what you did! I've got my own problems! Joshua wants to take me to the Thanksgiving dance, and I know Daddy won't let me go. If I can't go, I know Joshua will take somebody else!" She had the hiccups. "And Saundra is mad at me!"

"What about me, Sienna? You're so wrapped up in some stupid boy, you can't see anything! Uncle Ben just left! Daddy made him go!" Charlie shouted, "I keep your secrets. Why didn't you help me?"

The rain pounded the roof that evening. Charlie packed away the business supplies and gave Popcorn a bath. She stood in the deserted kitchen, staring out at the rock. Where was Uncle Ben? What a mess she'd made!

Eleven

Noises disturbed Charlie. Sienna was throwing clothes and shoes about, muttering and fussing. Popcorn licked Charlie on the corner of her mouth. Twice. Groaning, Charlie rubbed her eyes, parts of the dream still jumbled up inside.

Sienna stood in the middle of the room, breathing heavily, both hands on her hips. "I want to know where my navy blue sweater with the pink flowers is!"

Charlie yawned. "I don't know." The last time she had seen that particular sweater, it was in Popcorn's mouth as he dragged it under her bed.

"If I find out that you took my sweater, you're in trouble! And do something with your stinky dog!" Sienna stormed out of the room.

"Shoot, I'm in trouble now," Charlie said. She shifted, stretched, then bent down and retrieved the sweater. One sleeve was wet. With care, Charlie wedged it at the foot of Sienna's cluttered bed and threw a blouse over the part that stuck out. That done, she dressed and had breakfast.

Expecting to hear from two people, Charlie hovered

near the telephone. She knew that Uncle Ben could take care of himself, but she wanted to know where he was. Strangely enough, she hoped he was with Dinah.

Katie Rose Bainbridge was another matter. She was mad at Katie Rose. When the time had come yesterday afternoon for Charlie to trek back to Mr. Rocker's office, she'd waited by her desk, hoping that Katie Rose would go with her. But Katie Rose had chosen instead to duck her head and fiddle around in her desk. They both knew it had been pure luck that Katie Rose had taken a bathroom break at the exact moment the teacher's aide happened by.

Watching the telephone, Charlie had to admit she had known from the beginning that Katie Rose lacked real daring. And her partner had been honest about that and about her unwillingness to get into any trouble. But there was something called friendship. . . . "A real friend would serve detention with me, Popcorn!"

The door buzzer rang, and Mama let Granddad and Mama Bliss in. In minutes they had ushered Charlie and Sienna out of the house. The idea was for neither of them to be there when Oscar returned from grocery shopping and getting his hair cut.

"Your grandfather and I drew broom straws. He lost and got stuck with Sienna." Mama Bliss chuckled.

Charlie knew that Mama had done what the Pippins always did in a family emergency: call for the troops to gather. That explained why her grandparents had shown up ready to divide the sisters and take them for the day. Pouting, Sienna had flounced off to her grandfather's blue station wagon.

"I can't put up with girls wailing and acting like a fool over some boy! Humph! Next month Sienna will be moaning about a new love." With a hard foot down on the clutch, Mama Bliss shifted, then increased speed.

"Uncle Ben hasn't called yet. Do you think he's all right?" asked Charlie.

"Ben is not going to get lost trying to find himself," said Mama Bliss gruffly. "Of course he's fine. Reach in my purse and pull out my list. We've got things to do, Charlie."

The large leather purse that her grandmother usually carried slung over her right shoulder like a hobo's pack lay in the backseat on top of the plaid blanket. Charlie found pencils, pens, sketches of bottle designs, an overdue water bill, two old Christmas cards from last year, three rolls of quarters, one roll of dimes, a photo of her grandfather, and, finally, the sought-after list scrawled on the back of an envelope.

"Got it!" she announced.

Mama Bliss winked.

The sun never came out that day. When most of it had passed, running errands with Mama Bliss, stopping for bathroom breaks, grabbing a quick lunch, and driving across the freezing Golden Gate Bridge, the article about her father began to feel heavy in her pants pocket. Charlie huddled under the blanket as the red towers of the Golden Gate Bridge soared above her.

"Mama Bliss, was Daddy a hero in Vietnam?"

"They said so and gave him a bronze star, some other medals, and a citation. I was just glad he came back alive. Humph. Talk about sending an angel to wipe the lion's mouth. That war was the lion's mouth. You've got that look, Charlie. What's going on?"

Looking at Mama Bliss, Charlie remembered other photographs she had uncovered in the pages of the shabby album. One showed Daddy returned from war, still in uniform, and Mama Bliss, younger then, wearing her hair short and curled, rested against him. Her dark arms were wrapped around his waist, tight around his waist as if she'd never let him go. The medals lay pinned to his uniform right above her head. Charlie wondered where they were. Had her father kept them?

The second photo had been taken at a beach. Mama Bliss held her father's hand as they played in the ocean. The water swirled around his fat, toddler thighs.

Charlie made a decision. "I found this, by accident, in one of your old albums."

Glancing over, her grandmother took the newspaper article.

"Mama Bliss, I never saw Daddy cry," Charlie said.

"No. He was never a crier. Even when your father hurt himself as a little boy, he didn't cry much. Lord knows, with all he got into and as many times as he came home bleeding from one knock or another, he should have let more tears out. What do you really want to know, Charlie?" she asked, now driving through San Francisco, bound for home across the Bay.

Questions tumbled out. "Mama Bliss, what did Daddy want to be? What was his old dream? Where are his medals? What should I do with the article? Should I let him know I've read it? Why won't you or Mama tell me anything?"

Surprised, Charlie watched her grandmother hand the article back to her. Mama Bliss said nothing. She regarded Charlie silently. Her eyes shone like two new pennies, and a smile lifted the corners of her mouth. Then she reached over, tweaked a ponytail, and hit the accelerator. Charlie sighed, thinking that her life had been simpler before she'd found the newspaper article.

When her grandmother turned into the space in front of the garage behind her grandfather's car, Charlie hopped out. Granddad was coming down the steps.

"Did you have a good time?" he asked.

"I'm pooped. Mama Bliss had fifty errands to do. Sometimes I think she saves them up until she can kidnap me," Charlie replied.

"How did you ever figure that out?" he said, moving past her to speak to Mama Bliss.

Charlie stood on the steps, watching them. "Understanding the two of you is impossible, too!" she murmured as they kissed.

The brown shingled house was empty, except for Sheba and Popcorn, and Sienna, who was sulking in front of the television, her stationery on the cocktail table. Charlie wrinkled her pug nose at her sister. Then she heard the phone ring and ran to answer it.

"Charlie, hi, it's me, Katie Rose."

"Hi."

"Did you get in a lot of trouble?" she asked.

"Do dogs bark? Daddy got so mad at everybody that he made Uncle Ben move out for driving us to school. He called my grandmother and told her off for giving us paints. And Sienna got grounded."

There was a long silence.

"I feel bad, Charlie. I mean, I should have gotten caught, too. Do you want the money back?" she asked.

Charlie waited to hear more, but Katie Rose was silent. "No, you earned that. Look, I've got to go. See you later." Charlie hung up before Katie Rose could answer. At least she could have said something about Charlie's doing detention alone!

Charlie jumped up and took Popcorn for a run down the block. On the way there, she said, "Katie Rose and I are different, Popcorn. I take chances. She runs from them. Her parents are divorced. Mine aren't. She has an older brother at college. Lucky me, I've got Sienna at home. I've got business experience. She has none. Shoot, I refuse to add Katie Rose to my list of people to understand!"

That evening, Charlie's parents left the girls for dinner in San Francisco at their favorite Italian restaurant. Then they were going to a jazz club to hear Lewis Jordan and his group.

After they'd left, Charlie wandered around, searching for something to do. The thought of homework made her sick. Origami was a painful reminder of being out of business. There weren't any new library books to read.

Then the telephone rang, and Charlie hoped it was the other call she wanted. She rushed to get it before Sienna could.

"Charlie, hi, it's your uncle," the voice said.

"Uncle Ben! Are you all right? Where are you staying? When am I going to see you?" The questions came out faster than he could answer them.

Charlie listened and wrote down the information he

gave her. He was renting a motel room on the outskirts of San Francisco until he could find an apartment.

"Uncle Ben, do you have enough money? Are you lonely? I mean, I hope you and Dinah go out."

He reassured her. "Thanks for asking, Charlie. I've got most of the bonus I got from my last job. And Dinah helps me a lot, so I'm not lonely. I'm doing fine."

Over breakfast on Sunday, Charlie told her parents where Uncle Ben was. Her father lifted his eyes from the paper.

"Oh, I thought he'd stay with Dinah," said Mama, eyes half-shut with sleep.

"Looks like one of them has sense. I don't approve of living together," her father said. "Either get married or go your separate ways."

"Daddy, everybody is living together!" Sienna chimed in.

"When did everybody doing anything make it right?" he bellowed.

Sienna was quick to agree. Charlie couldn't believe her sister was dumb enough to say something like that.

"And, Sienna, I want you to spend less time writing Joshua and more time studying." His voice was low and angry.

By Monday morning, Charlie had resigned herself to weeks of detention. When she saw Chris and Katie Rose, she lapsed into silence.

As soon as class started, Mrs. Hayamoto asked for volunteers to compete in the District Oratory Contest. First there would be a competition held among the students in their room. The winner would compete against the other three sixth-grade classes for the honor of representing Hayden at the district level. Katie Rose whispered that she was too shy. Chris wasn't interested. He was caught up in a new project, preparing for the spring science fair.

"Chartreuse, why don't I see your hand up? I'm putting your name down. And I expect you to turn that excellent report into a winning speech." Although Mrs. Hayamoto smiled, Charlie knew she was serious. So she raised her hand and agreed.

"You want me to help you practice for the contest?" offered Katie Rose.

"No, thanks." Although it was difficult to turn away in the crowded cluster, Charlie struggled.

"Charlie, what do you want me to do? Turn myself in?" Katie Rose looked ready to burst into tears. Her voice quivered. Red splotches covered her face. Her forehead wrinkled up.

"I don't want to talk about it," whispered Charlie, making sure that Mrs. Hayamoto's back was turned toward the low math group. "Detention is no big deal. I'll survive, Katie Rose. This isn't worth crying about."

"Charlie, my mother is falling apart. If I go to Rocker and tell him to put me on detention with you, she'll start crying about how the divorce is destroying both of us." The urgency in Katie Rose's face forced Chris to peer at the two girls over his stack of books on electricity. "She'll ship me off to some psychiatrist! Call another meeting with my father, and they'll scream at each other. I can't take any more of that!"

Charlie stared at her, feeling both sorry and disappointed.

"Here's the money." Katie Rose handed over a brown envelope, containing her 40 percent of the profits from the Halloween business. But Charlie shoved it back across their desks.

"Look, forget it, Katie Rose. I should never have asked you."

At the end of the school day, Chris headed home, while Katie Rose slipped away to catch the bus to her father's. Charlie peeked in to the library to see where she would be serving her daily hour of detention starting tomorrow.

One afternoon that same week, while the early November rain pummeled the high library windows, her father entered the quiet room. Only five children were there. The librarian was cataloging books in the back room.

"Come on, Charlie," he said. The water dripped from his hat and raincoat. "We'll put your bike in the car."

"I brought my rain slicker and hat, Daddy," she said.

"Riding that bike in this weather is too dangerous. I figured you planned to do that. Your mother called me at work. She'll be late, so let's go to the store. Sienna can make a tuna fish casserole."

They didn't talk much, but, then, they never did, not conversation talk where one person shared and the other person listened, then shared and waited patiently. But at the supermarket Charlie decided to try. What could she lose?

"I'm not selling anything anymore, Daddy." Charlie selected two large cans of albacore tuna and dropped them into the cart.

"About time."

"And Mrs. Hayamoto personally asked me to compete in the District Oratory Contest. I can earn back some of the points I lost as a 'responsible learner.'" Charlie had to force the last sentence out.

He paused. "We had those when I went to school. Had to memorize speeches by famous Black orators. I remember one your mother delivered by Sojourner Truth called 'Ain't I a Woman!'" He threw a large package of sharp cheddar cheese into the cart.

"I'm going to write my own speech, about ideas I believe in," Charlie said.

He laughed the same hard way he had about the rock in the backyard. "Believing in what you're saying won't guarantee winning."

"Daddy, I'd never spit on any soldier," she said, the words out before she thought. "I don't believe in acting like that!"

"So you heard about that? I never thought I'd have a peace nut in my house." He shook his head.

"But I'm not a peace nut, Daddy!" Charlie pushed the grocery cart to the side of the aisle, making room for a heavyset woman and two children. She thought of Akima and the man who'd told her those horrible things. "What's so wrong about me speaking out?"

"Because you don't understand what you're saying," he shouted, causing the woman to glare at them. "Sometimes war is necessary. So is killing. Don't look at me like that. I don't mean nuclear war."

"But, Daddy—" she started.

"No more buts," he ordered, shoving the cart forward.

Inside, Charlie felt a new resolve. Her father was wrong! She had a right to speak out!

That evening, while the cheese bubbled on the tuna casserole, Charlie called Mama Bliss. After the conversation, she told her father that she would be going to help her grandmother after detention for the next week. He nodded.

Charlie had struggled to find a way to transform the report on Vietnam into a winning speech. When the answer had come, she'd slapped her forehead. The key was to integrate her report with what she'd learned about war and peace from Katie Rose and Chris. Then she'd have to come up with ideas about the way people should live to make peace a real possibility for her generation.

Charlie had set to work, talking with her friends and whittling down the pages of statistics and facts into a speech. She called it "A New Way of Thinking."

Now she was ready for the first oratory practice sessions with her grandparents. The two of them sat on the sofa in Mama Bliss's living room, listening. Granddad's golden eyes were fixed on her as Mama Bliss jumped up and down and hollered, "No! No! No! Charlie, make those sentences simpler. Think about what this new way of thinking is."

Charlie was exhausted. It was the ninth time they'd gone over this part. She crossed out the words on the card and rewrote them. "Okay, listen to this: In my new way of thinking, we believe that peace begins with each individual family. We value and encourage the participation of children working for peace. And, finally, we do everything possible to stop the production of nuclear weapons and to get rid of the ones we have."

"Remember to pause. Enunciate clearly and look strong," Mama Bliss instructed. "We'll all be there watching you, rebel."

Charlie bit her lip. Her father wouldn't like any of this. She hoped he wouldn't come.

Not long after, Charlie delivered her speech in the classroom, easily defeating her competition. Chris shook her hand. And when Katie Rose held out her hand, Charlie shook it. Afterward, Mrs. Hayamoto moved the name Chartreuse Marie Pippin up two slots. In spite of herself, Charlie smiled. She hated to be at the bottom of anything, even the Discipline Code chart, especially when Katie Rose's name was near the top.

Finally, the day of the Hayden Elementary School oratory contest arrived. Both of her grandparents showed up to hear her. When Charlie faced the other three sixth-grade competitors in the school auditorium, her heart raced. But she held her head high and delivered a victorious speech. Granddad and Mama Bliss applauded long after everyone had stopped. Next time Charlie would be representing all of the sixth-graders at Hayden in the District Oratory Contest. She had barely two weeks to prepare.

There was one special person she wanted to share the news with, but it was impossible lately to get Uncle Ben on the phone. He was either at his new job or out with Dinah.

If Charlie didn't think of calling her father, Mr. Rocker did. The principal called Mr. Pippin at work and told him how proud the entire school was that Charlie had won.

And Mrs. Hayamoto phoned the house that night to congratulate Charlie's mother.

"I'm really proud of you, Charlie," Mrs. Pippin said. "Sienna, get in here. Your sister is famous! Charlie, why didn't you tell us?"

The oak logs in the fireplace crackled and blazed, heating the living room. Popcorn and Sheba were curled up on either side of the cocktail table, too full and sleepy to fight. Tugging a towel tightly around her wet hair, Sienna posed by the dining room table.

"I just thought that if I didn't win, there wouldn't be anything to tell," said Charlie, eyeing the fire.

"So this is what you meant about entering an oratory contest?" her father asked.

"Oscar, don't pour cold water on this. Charlie has done something positive. Obviously Mr. Rocker and Mrs. Hayamoto believe that what she said has value," interrupted Mrs. Pippin. "And so do the judges."

"That's nice, Charlie. Maybe you'll end up being a politician or a peace demonstrator." Sienna sauntered back to the bathroom.

"Shut up, Sienna!" she called.

Charlie watched her father leave.

"That husband of mine!" Mrs. Pippin hugged Charlie, "Don't mind him, Charlie. I'm really proud of you. He is, too."

After taking Popcorn for a run outside, she led him around to the backyard. The night air was cold but dry. Clambering up the rock, Charlie considered the possibility that her father might show up at the District Oratory Contest, then dismissed it. She wondered if she could stand before hundreds of strangers and deliver a winning speech. She felt in her jacket pocket for the newspaper article. In the strangest way, the words and photograph had become a friend, reminding her that there was work left to do. How long could she keep it in her pocket?

Twelve

Thanksgiving was celebrated in traditional Pippin style. The entire family was there, and for the first time since he'd moved out, Charlie saw Uncle Ben. She'd looked forward to meeting Dinah, but at the last minute a tour guide had gotten the flu and Dinah had had to replace him on a tour to Italy.

Uncle Ben seemed changed, quieter and more serious. He spoke of something he had to do in Washington, D.C., adding that he might be seeing Aunt Jessie real soon. But he refused to elaborate. So Charlie made sure that Uncle Ben heard her say she really wanted to see Aunt Jessie. She could only hope that he got the hint.

During the toasts and laughter, Charlie wondered how Katie Rose was handling her first Thanksgiving with divorced parents. She gazed around the dining room table, glad to see her family gathered together, laughing and talking and eating and enjoying the holiday.

After dinner there were more good times. Daddy set up the card tables, and games of bid whist and Crazy Eights got going. Around ten P.M., Daddy put on some music and asked Mama to dance. Charlie grinned when Uncle Ben invited her at the same time that Granddad reached for Mama Bliss's hand. Sienna had disappeared down the hall to the telephone. By the time Charlie collapsed into bed, she was filled with food and good family memories.

First thing the next morning, Charlie called Katie Rose. "Hi, I just wanted to find out how your Thanksgiving went," she said.

"Terrible. Dad's got a girlfriend, a real dimwit. She's young enough to be my older sister, about twenty-two. She giggles, tosses her hair around, and wears red nail polish with glitter," reported Katie Rose, keeping her voice down.

"Your mother's home?" asked Charlie.

"In her bedroom. She called yesterday and Blondie— that's what I call her—had the nerve to answer the phone while Dad was in the kitchen. Mother grilled me all night about who the woman was, what she looked like, how did Dad treat her. Look, Charlie, I can't talk now."

"I'm sorry, Katie Rose. I don't know what to say. Want to meet around eleven and go get some ice cream?" she asked.

"You mean it, Charlie? I figured you'd never want to be friends again. Great. Let's meet in front of Baskin-Robbins on Shattuck Avenue."

Riding her bicycle on a cold November day with piles of leaves lining the sidewalk and the sun crystal-bright felt good. Charlie loved the power of her muscular legs pushing the pedals up and down, accelerating the bike forward into new space. Charlie sniffed the Berkeley, California, air and thought of the coming winter rainstorms.

When she got to the store, Katie Rose was waiting, her blue bike securely locked to a parking meter. "I'll treat," Katie Rose announced, unzipping her down jacket. "That's the very least a coward like me can do."

Taken aback, Charlie locked her bike and said nothing.

Katie Rose insisted that they order triple scoops. She asked for a sugar cone with one scoop of Chocolate Comet, a mixture of dark chocolate, marshmallow, and raspberry swirls. Then she added a scoop of Nutty Coconut and another of Peanut Butter n' Chocolate.

Charlie gulped. "Just three scoops of Chocolate Chip in a cup for me."

They sat in the pink plastic seats that lined the room. For a while they ate in silence.

"I decided to use the money I made helping you with the face painting business to treat us." The loneliness in Katie Rose's blue eyes jarred Charlie. "I know I'm a coward to you for not going to Rocker and confessing that I was part of the business. I'm a coward and not much of a friend."

"Well," said Charlie, "I do feel bad because you're letting me take the punishment alone. But it *was* my idea. I persuaded you to get involved. And you told me how scared you were."

"No, you never forced me, Charlie. I wanted to. Being in business is exciting! I had fun, real fun for the first time in months!" She took a long lick of Nutty Coconut.

"Being in business causes problems," Charlie said thoughtfully. "I feel bad about getting my uncle Ben in trouble. Selling stuff at school wasn't too smart." She sighed. "I love selling products and stamping my name on receipts. But I'll have to figure out a way that keeps me on the good side of Daddy and Mr. Rocker. Then it'll be okay for you, too."

Katie Rose got teary-eyed.

Charlie laughed. "Okay. Let's just forget what happened. As long as you treat me to ice cream!" Then Katie Rose laughed.

The girls unlocked their bikes and rode back to Charlie's house. Everybody was out. The afternoon sun sank much too quickly, sliding away while they listened to records and played Scrabble.

The District Oratory Contest was held the following Wednesday evening in a crowded high school auditorium. Scanning the rows before her from the high stage, Charlie located Mama, Granddad, Mama Bliss, Uncle Ben, and Sienna. Next to Sienna there was an empty seat. Charlie was glad Daddy hadn't come.

Mama Bliss gave her the raised fist sign. Sienna crooked a finger. Mrs. Hayamoto waved at Charlie from the front row, next to Katie Rose and Chris.

The stage was filled with two rows of folding chairs, where the winners from each school were seated. Charlie assessed her competition: a grave Black girl from Ellis Elementary and a white boy from Williams Elementary. The boy seemed as nervous as Charlie felt.

Breathing deeply, Charlie smoothed her blue paisley dress. But she frowned at her white knee-high socks and flat shoes. The other girl had on real stockings and shoes with a heel. Charlie's thick, long hair was in a ponytail twisted into a ball on top of her head. Her opponent's was curled in the newest fashion.

It was time for the contest to begin. After his principal introduced him, the boy walked to the podium and waited for the applause to stop. While he spoke, Charlie witnessed a transformation. The anxious boy turned into a polished speaker who delivered a well-rehearsed speech about energy conservation.

"The next speaker is Chartreuse Marie Pippin, representing the sixth-grade classes at Hayden Elementary School. Miss Pippin is a student in Mrs. Hayamoto's room," said Mr. Rocker. "The title of her speech is 'A New Way of Thinking.'" Charlie tried to grin when he gave her the thumbs-up sign. She knew he wanted her to win first place.

Following the coaching instructions from her grandparents, Charlie surveyed the audience and planted her feet firmly on the wooden platform, lifting her head high. Each candidate had a maximum of fifteen minutes to speak. She arranged her numbered index cards and began.

"Good evening, fellow students, parents, teachers, and administrators. I am honored to be here tonight. I come from a family that has a long, proud, and distinguished history of fighting for America. Both of my grandfathers fought in World War II. My father and my uncle fought in Vietnam and were wounded. I am very proud of them, and I love them. I don't agree with my father or uncle. Going to war in Vietnam was wrong. War is wrong. I come before you to urge that we learn to think in a new way—a way that means peace. After reading, thinking, learning from my classmates, Katie Rose Bainbridge and

Chris Saunders, and listening to family discussions, I believe that the only way children will have the chance to grow up, instead of being blown up, is if we think, act, and live in peace."

The auditorium was still. Charlie paused and looked from her left to her right, taking in her teacher's encouraging smile and the nod from her mother.

"In my new way of thinking, we believe that peace begins with each individual family. We encourage children and adults to work for peace. We do everything possible to stop the production of nuclear weapons and get rid of the ones we have. Why? Because we commit ourselves to a safe future for all children by cleaning up our home, this planet." Applause started, so Charlie waited until it had died down. Inside she felt excited. The speech was getting off to a wonderful start!

"I began by learning about one war, the Vietnam War, the only war that the United States lost and the longest one we fought. Ten years after the fall of Saigon, there is still anger and bitterness about America's involvement in a civil war thousands of miles away. In my home, my father and my uncle still argue about going there and about the thousands of Black infantrymen killed in Vietnam, far more than was just. In the newspapers I read about veterans who are still sick and in need of help, about men and women never properly welcomed home."

Just then Charlie saw her father stride down the long aisle, searching for the family. She gulped. How could he be here?

"In Washington, D.C., there is a long, black granite wall, the Vietnam Memorial. On that wall are engraved thousands of names of the dead from Vietnam. In our new way of thinking there would never be another wall like that." Charlie lost her place and skipped the part where she was supposed to tell what she had learned from Chris's report. In fumbling through her cards, she dropped the one that listed the facts about nuclear war she'd gotten from Katie Rose. She bent down to pick it up. When she stood up again, she saw frowns on Daddy's face and her teacher's.

"Excuse me," she said. "A new way of thinking means that we reduce the fifty thousand nuclear weapons to none. That we must accept the horrible fact that no one will survive a nuclear war. Uh . . . uh . . ." Charlie searched for the next card. Somehow they'd gotten out of order. She couldn't stand there in front of five hundred people and reorder them. She'd just have to fake it.

"A single, one-megaton nuclear bomb would wipe out this auditorium, our families, and homes. Children know this and the ones I talked to are afraid and angry because adults won't stop this . . . this insanity. Their families won't even talk about nuclear war with . . . with . . . them." Charlie faltered again. "That's why children have to take the lead. Their opinions have to be . . . uh . . . uh . . . respected and listened to by their mothers and . . ."— Charlie saw her father shake his head—"and fathers. Peace talk begins in the home, around the kitchen table. Then we need to learn more about war and peace in school. When a seven-year-old girl tells me she's scared because 'they' are going to push a button and kill everything—" Charlie stopped and stared down. The next card listed facts about Vietnam! As she searched frantically for the right one, the stack slid off the podium and scattered at her feet! The rubber band in her stomach snapped so hard, it was difficult to draw a breath.

Now the audience was beginning to fidget. Fighting the tears that filled her eyes, Charlie stared at her grandfather and grandmother. "Excuse me. When I listen to a twelve-year-old boy say he knows that he'll never be thirty or get married or even go on a date because of nuclear war, then I know that we have to think in a new way." Just then she felt a short burst of courage and said firmly, "Earth is home to all of us. Young and old. Black and white. Rich and poor. Communist and noncommunist. All of us. Thank you."

Biting her lip and swallowing hard, Charlie fought the tears that threatened to spill over. The applause resounded, but she knew that she'd lost critical points. That reality was driven home when the other Black girl finished a speech about stopping drug and alcohol abuse without making a single error. From the first syllable to the last, she exuded passion and power. The boy gazed over at Charlie and closed his eyes. They both knew that the girl strutting back to her chair with a grin that spread from California to Connecticut would walk away with the blue and gold first-place ribbon.

Charlie knew she could have beaten her, if only she hadn't been shaken by the sight of her father. Why did he have to come and spoil everything?

The winners were announced. As Charlie accepted the handshakes and the plain blue ribbon that said THIRD PLACE, she wanted to throw herself down and kick and scream and cry her heart out.

Katie Rose and Chris were the first to reach her. "Charlie, that was an intelligent, inspirational speech. You expressed valuable ideas," Chris said, patting her on the shoulder.

"I'd never have the nerve to get up in front of all these people and talk," said Katie Rose, her eyes sympathetic and the touch of her hand on Charlie's hand comforting. "I'm proud to be your friend, Charlie. Real proud."

"Thanks, but you two know I should have done better! I skipped so much stuff." The tears started to well again, and this time Charlie swiped at them.

"What's this crying, rebel?" came her grandmother's husky voice.

Charlie couldn't hold back anymore. "I'm so sorry, Mama Bliss. I know you wanted me to win. You and granddad spent all that time, and I came in last!"

Mama Bliss shushed her, wiping at Charlie's face with the edge of her wool scarf.

"And you think that's why we helped you, so you could win first place?" her grandfather asked.

Instead of answering, Charlie buried her head in her grandmother's coat.

"We helped you because we want you to be able to speak your mind in a civilized way," he said. "And you did that."

By then the rest of the Pippin family had gathered and Chris and Katie Rose had left. Charlie dried her eyes and stood back, accepting hugs and congratulations from her mother and uncle. Even Sienna commented on how nice the ribbon was.

But when she faced her father, Charlie felt sick to her

stomach. She realized how important winning first place had been. Charlie took off the third-place ribbon.

"If you earn something like that, you should wear it, Charlie," her father said.

"It's not first place!" she muttered, pulling on the coat that her sister handed her.

The car ride home was quiet. There was no triumphant celebration at an ice cream store. She huddled in the backseat.

Once home, Charlie took two aspirins with a glass of milk.

"No sense getting all upset," her father said. "You tried. But I don't agree with what you said. Children aren't grown enough to solve adult problems."

That was too much for Charlie. "You spoiled everything for me! Just like you always do! And why should I wear my ribbon? You never even show your medals from Vietnam, Daddy!"

"What in the world are you talking about?" he demanded.

"I was doing fine until I saw you! But I knew you'd get mad if you heard my speech and I got—" Charlie stopped, not wanting to say the next word out loud. "Scared. I got too scared to say my speech."

"That's not fair, Charlie," said her mother. "Your father came to support you!"

"How do you know about my medals?" he asked.

"I don't know," mumbled Charlie, too exhausted to fight anymore. "I guess I saw a picture somewhere."

Her parents asked in unison, "Where?"

Charlie started to cry. "I don't remember. What does

that matter? I lost!" Without waiting for them to reply, she pushed past Sienna and locked herself in the bathroom.

Grateful that they hadn't followed her, Charlie stood in front of the mirror. She looked pitiful! Just like a third-place loser. After hours of research and practice, her father had made her lose. She ran cold water on a washcloth and patted her face. She looked hard at herself, now seeing the hard truth. Her father hadn't made her lose. He'd thought enough to come. She'd made herself lose because she couldn't say what she believed in front of her father without falling apart.

Bedtime came. Outside Sienna's window the deserted hummingbird feeder swung in the cold wind. The fog had rolled in. Charlie reached over Popcorn to turn off her desk lamp. Her hand brushed the article, which lay on top of the *National Geographic*. With her usual care, Charlie placed the article under her pillow and switched off the light. How could she figure out what to do with her father's secrets, secrets that had become her own?

Thirteen

During the dark night, Charlie awoke. Popcorn was sleeping on his back. She propped herself up on one elbow and found Sienna sitting up in bed, staring out the window.

"Your headache gone?" asked Sienna, stroking her cat.

"Yes. Why are you awake?"

"Can't sleep." Charlie could tell that something was wrong. Normally Sienna snored through the night like a log, bobbing along in her bed.

"I'm going to get something to drink." Without disturbing her dog, Charlie rolled out of bed, slipped into warm slippers, and grabbed a quilted robe. Daddy turned the heat down at night to save on the high cost of electricity.

The hallway was darker than the bedroom. The door to her parents' bedroom was tightly closed. Charlie tiptoed into the kitchen. There was a light under the stove that she turned on. Popcorn trotted in, yawning, with Sheba behind him.

After pouring herself a glass of milk and cutting a chunk

of cheddar cheese to go with crackers, Charlie let both pets out the back door and sat down to eat. Before she could take a bite, Sienna moseyed in. Charlie watched her sister make a cup of tea and add four teaspoonfuls of sugar.

Again Sienna startled her. With a heavy groan, Sienna sank into the kitchen chair next to Charlie, then roused herself to let the animals in. "Fifteen feels awful," she said. "When I was eleven, like you, my life was so easy. I went to school, acted like a good girl, and played with my little girlfriends."

"Come off it, Sienna. There's only four years' difference between eleven and fifteen. You talk like you're as old as Mama Bliss!" sputtered Charlie.

"You just wait until you're fifteen, Charlie. Four years is an eternity! Your life isn't nearly as complicated as mine."

"I give up. What's bothering you?"

"You wouldn't understand! Nobody does. Not even Mama. Daddy hollers at me just like he does you. I never believed that could happen." Sienna rested her head on the table. "When we run he doesn't talk to me anymore. I'm bored with running, anyway."

Charlie cut a pie-shaped wedge of cheddar cheese and placed it on a cracker.

"You don't have to ignore me, too. I'm in the middle of a disaster, Charlie! I have the biggest decision of my life to make." Sienna blew her nose. "Saundra likes Joshua. What am I supposed to do? Give up Joshua because Saundra has the nerve to like him?"

Charlie was dumbfounded. "Saundra's your best friend,

Sienna! You wouldn't choose a boy over her? And who does Joshua like best? You or Saundra?"

Sienna closed her eyes. "That's what I mean. You don't understand! Nobody does!" Blowing her nose fiercely, she dragged herself out of the kitchen.

While Charlie chewed on her cheese and crackers, she thought about facing her classmates in a few hours. Sienna couldn't imagine what a complicated life *she* had.

Thursday morning, Charlie selected a fire-engine red outfit to lift her spirits. She squared her shoulders and gave herself one last firm look in the mirror before leaving for school.

As Mrs. Hayamoto announced the results of the oratory contest, Charlie met the eyes of the children around her. They clapped politely. She raised her chin. But even though she braved her way through the morning, she felt terrible. Winning third place felt worse than not winning at all. And losing her nerve felt even worse than that!

That afternoon, the class learned that one of the project committees wanted to have a bake sale to raise money for the African relief fund. Being in business was a part of her. This might be the way—the legal way—to get back into it. Charlie raised her hand. She asked if the class could sell other things besides cookies, cakes, and pies.

"What do you mean, Chartreuse?" asked Mrs. Hayamoto.

It was time to think fast. "Why don't we have a holiday bazaar and sell a variety of products. I could sell my origami animals. I know that my grandmother would be willing to donate some of her tree bottles," Charlie said, her eyes shining.

"And I could paint faces," added Katie Rose in a small but clear voice.

"Oh?" Mrs. Hayamoto's eyes narrowed. "I didn't know you knew how to paint faces, Kathryn Rose."

Charlie grimaced, hoping Katie Rose wouldn't choose now to make a stand.

"Yes, I do know how. And Mrs. Hayamoto—"

Before she could finish, Charlie interrupted. "And I bet other kids in here have ideas for things to sell. We could hold the holiday bazaar on a Saturday, when people with money, like our parents, could come," she joked, looking at Chris for support.

Chris took the cue. "Frankly, Mrs. Hayamoto, this is a sound suggestion that has economic potential. We could make our bazaar a biannual event focusing on the appropriate holidays and involve the larger school community." He turned around and threw Charlie a conspiratorial smile.

Katie Rose swallowed. "Sure. This year we could focus on Christmas, Hanukkah, the Chinese New Year, and other holidays celebrated around the end of the year. Call it the Winter Holiday Bazaar!"

"And we could have another one in the spring!" Charlie said.

That sparked an enthusiastic discussion. Within the hour, instead of a bake sale, the project committees had decided to cooperate to run a Winter Holiday Bazaar.

But something bothered Charlie. Up shot her hand.

"Chartreuse, what else?" said her teacher.

"Well, I think we should be allowed to keep a portion of the profits. I mean, to encourage . . ." She paused, unsure of how to say what she wanted to without appearing greedy.

"To encourage a spirit of entrepreneurship," interjected Chris, flourishing his mechanical pencil.

"And to encourage kids to work hard and stay involved," added Katie Rose.

Mrs. Hayamoto cleared her throat and pointed at Charlie. "Chartreuse, are you suggesting that the best way to motivate your classmates is with money?"

Chris spoke up. "No, but it helps."

The class laughed.

"What about the costs of supplies? Face paints and glitter cost money. So does origami paper," Katie Rose said.

The teacher rested against her desk, arms crossed, eyes focused on Charlie.

"Look, I'm used to being in business and making a profit. Part goes into a savings account, part pays for materials, and some of the rest goes for jewelry," Charlie admitted. "I figured that keeping some of the money would give everyone a chance to experience—"

"Getting rich!" yelled someone.

"Being a capitalist!" another student said.

Charlie stood up. "No! Look, I'll participate even if we vote to donate all the money. But running a real business means making a profit for yourself."

A heated discussion followed, with some kids arguing for donating everything to hungry people and others taking the position that a small profit would encourage participation. Then the class compromised. Sellers could keep 10 percent of the money they made above supply costs or donate all of it to the bazaar. Charlie chose not to engage in the debate. She had said enough.

The Winter Holiday Bazaar would be held in the school gym in two weeks. Together Charlie and Katie Rose volunteered to be on the publicity committee. Painting posters and stapling them up around school sounded like more fun than work.

After serving detention, Charlie hurried home. It was really too late to be of any help in her grandfather's store.

The house was empty, so she turned on the thermostat and let Popcorn out. Anxious, Charlie watched the clock and listened for the sound of her sister. Just as her mother opened the front door, Sienna telephoned.

"You'd better beat Daddy home, Sienna. Mama just came in. What do you want me to say?"

"Tell Mama I had to stay late for cheerleading practice. Charlie, please, I have to wait until basketball practice is over to talk to Joshua. 'Bye."

"Who was that, sugar?" Mrs. Pippin was headed for her bedroom to change and meditate.

"Sienna. She has to stay late for cheerleading practice," Charlie lied.

Mrs. Pippin halted. "Are you telling me the truth, Charlie?"

"No, Mama. She's going to see Joshua after basketball practice. Sienna's life is like a soap opera."

"Come here and tell me about this little soap opera," said her mother, pushing Charlie into the kitchen and into a chair.

"Sienna and Saundra are best friends," said Charlie. "Sienna likes Joshua. Joshua likes Sienna. Saundra likes Joshua."

"Promise me one thing, Charlie. When you get to be fifteen, you won't act like your sister." Mrs. Pippin heated water in the tea kettle.

"If she doesn't beat Daddy home, he'll kill her."

"Maybe she needs to get caught by him," mused Mrs. Pippin. "Let's talk about something happy. All day long I thought about your speech. I know you didn't say everything you planned to, but there you were, my baby, standing up in front of five hundred people, speaking up for the men in our family and at the same time practicing your own voice. My, my. I'm proud of you."

"I don't understand, Mama. I lost."

"Not in my eyes you didn't. You were being your own person, like that girl Akima you told me about," she said. "I wish my older daughter would show some sign of doing that."

The ringing telephone interrupted them. Charlie answered it.

"Rebel, good. I've got orders pouring in from the stores for more Christmas bottles! I need your help this Saturday. I'll throw in pizza and Scrabble," said Mama Bliss, her voice popping across the telephone like electrical sparks.

There was no way that Charlie could refuse. Mama Bliss had taken time to help her practice for the oratory contest. Time that she could have spent painting the bottles.

"Good. I'll pick you up about ten. Be ready. Now, let me talk to your mother."

The table was set, the dinner of chicken and dumplings ladled out, the glasses filled, the family seated, and grace said by the time Sienna opened the front door. She ran into the kitchen, panting. Rainwater dripped onto the polished linoleum floor.

"Where have you been?" her father asked. Charlie concentrated on eating her salad.

"I had to stay late for practice, but I hurried home. Hmm. That smells good. Hi, Mama. Be right back." Sienna turned, but not in time to elude his grasp.

"Not so fast, young lady. Today is Thursday. Your practice is on Tuesday," he said.

Charlie stared up at her silent, red-faced sister. Sienna was taking too long to answer. She'd better say something before he figured out that she was lying. But the quiet in the kitchen grew and grew, until Mr. Pippin pulled her down into a chair. Then, bit by bit, Charlie's parents drew the truth out of Sienna. Eventually the entire story lay on the table like a limp rope.

Just when the drama in the kitchen was reaching its peak, the telephone rang. Charlie answered it reluctantly, hoping it was a wrong number. She didn't want to miss a thing!

When she heard her uncle's voice, she was surprised. He hadn't been calling much lately. "Hi, Uncle Ben. You want to speak to Mama?" she asked.

"No, I called to talk to you. How are you doing?"

Charlie bit her lip, eager to get back, but happy to hear his voice. "Fine."

"I wanted to know if you'd like to fly to Washington, D.C., with me next weekend. We'd leave on Friday, stay with Aunt Jessie, and come back on Sunday," he said. "Dinah got me a great deal on airline tickets! Less than half-fare for me and practically nothing for you."

"What?" Charlie was flabbergasted, too shocked to reply. Deep disappointment washed over her. Daddy would never agree. Especially in the mood he was in now.

144

"First I want to know if you'd like to go. You said you would when we talked at Thanksgiving. And I need a way to thank you."

"Thank me?" Charlie asked, her interest in the drama in the kitchen fading fast.

"For the speech you gave at the oratory contest. You helped me take a big step," he explained.

"We could see the Vietnam Memorial? And Aunt Jessie? The statues, too?" she asked.

"You bet!"

"I really—I mean— Oh, yes, I want to go with you, Uncle Ben, but Daddy would never let me," she said.

"Is Oscar home?"

"Yeah."

"Let me talk to him."

"It won't work. I'll just get into trouble, Uncle Ben," she pleaded. "He's really mad right now. Not at me. At Sienna."

"Charlie, call your father to the phone. Please."

Instead she went for her mother, passing her sister in the hall.

Sienna blew her nose. "Daddy put me on punishment for the rest of the school year! Saundra's mad at me, and I can't go to the basketball game, anyway! I lost my best friend for nothing."

But Charlie was too busy rushing to call her mother to care. While her mother spoke to Uncle Ben, she joined her father at the table and took a mouthful of lukewarm broth. She got up to reheat hers, reaching for the other bowls.

"Thanks, Charlie." Her father ran his hand over his mustache. "Sienna lied. Well, I'm not going to accept that kind of behavior!" His voice rose.

Charlie saw that his train was stoking up coal, getting ready to head her way. She stirred the pot, her back to him.

"And you getting distraught over that contest! Acting like it was my fault you got third place! What did I do except rush from work, drive like a madman to get there in time to hear you?"

Yes, his train was rolling straight for her, Charlie decided. Fortunately, her mother returned before it could get too far.

"Good, Charlie. Thanks for reheating dinner," Mrs. Pippin said, sitting down. "What an evening this has turned into! Oscar, that was Ben."

"Mama, you want some more?" interrupted Charlie.

"Just half a bowl, please. Sit down here, Charlie. Oscar, Ben's got to go to Washington, D.C., a week from tomorrow and he wants to take Charlie with him. It would be just for the weekend," she said, patting her husband's hand.

"What?"

"Now, Oscar, I gave this some serious thought, and I think it would be a wonderful opportunity for Charlie. She'd get to visit with Jessie and see some of the things she studied about," said her mother. "And it'll be practically free, thanks to Dinah."

Charlie heard the sounds of water running. Sienna was taking a bath. Over her milk glass she stole a look at her father.

"I don't know, Ellie. Can't he go during her Christmas break?"

146

"No. Ben said this is the only time Dinah can get these airfares."

Charlie waited for her father's decision. When he looked at her, she looked back at him. "No. Call Ben and tell him maybe another time. Charlie, you're still on punishment. And I won't let you go while school is in session."

Charlie let out the breath she'd been holding, blinking back fat, hot tears.

"Please, Daddy, I really want to go. I've been good at school. You said that my report card was a lot better than last year's. I'm caught up in my work. Please, Daddy." She heard herself begging and crying at the same time. "I'll do double detention time."

"That's it! Now I've got two girls crying! Tell me, Ellie, why am I the bad guy? Just because I try to be the best father I can be?" He threw his napkin down on the table. "No! Just like I told Sienna, I'm telling you, Charlie. No!"

"Sugar, you call your uncle and tell him," her mother said over her shoulder as she hurried after Charlie's father.

For a long time, Charlie sat in the chair. When she went to bed that night, she still hadn't telephoned her uncle to tell him that she would not be flying to Washington, D.C., with him the following Friday. Instead, after Sienna was sound asleep, Charlie took out the *National Geographic* magazine and the newspaper article about her father. For the hundredth time, she examined the photographs in the glow of the lamplight. Suddenly, she knew she *had* to get to Washington, D.C. In that city was the best present she could give her father. But how could she get it when he refused to let her go?

Fourteen

Stumbling from the bathroom to the kitchen, Charlie yawned, barely noticing that it was a dry, sunny Saturday morning. The calendar on the wall said it was December seventh. She rubbed the sleep from her eyes. Mama bounced back and forth, singing. Sienna slept.

Charlie sat down at the kitchen table. Hearing her father's voice, she grunted and hastily scooped up the cereal that had missed the bowl when she'd poured it.

"Ellie, did you wash my gray sweat suit? I couldn't find it this morning," Mr. Pippin called from the bathroom.

"It's drying now, Oscar. By the way, Charlie, what did Ben say when you called him back yesterday?" Mrs. Pippin waited.

Charlie felt exactly the way Sienna had the night before last. Stuck. She lied. "Uncle Ben said we could go another time."

"I know you're disappointed, sugar, but Washington, D.C., isn't going anywhere. Maybe we'll go there next summer. When you finish up, help me in the living room,"

Mrs. Pippin said, moving on. "And we've got Christmas shopping to do when you get home!"

Before Mama Bliss came, while everyone was occupied elsewhere, Charlie made a phone call. She told her uncle that she had permission to go. Charlie explained that her father had agreed when she promised to make up any missed schoolwork, adding that Mama had fought for her to go with him. Uncle Ben believed her. He said that he'd be by to pick her up early Friday morning. That was six days away.

"How early, Uncle Ben?" Charlie asked.

"Our flight leaves at 10:10 A.M. from Oakland Airport, so we should get there by 9:15. I'll pick you up about eight. Here, take down the flight numbers and times for your mother."

Again, Charlie's mind calculated. Eight o'clock in the morning would just see both parents and Sienna out the front door. Unable to think of an alternative, Charlie quickly agreed. She jotted down the information and told her uncle she would call him on Wednesday to confirm.

One more possible snag occurred to her. "Does Aunt Jessie know about this trip? I mean, about me coming?"

"No, I haven't called her yet. Why don't we keep you a surprise? I'll fix it so Jessie thinks I'm coming alone!" He chuckled. "You know how your aunt loves the unexpected."

Faking a laugh, Charlie closed her eyes. Aunt Jessie would be on the phone talking to Mama ten seconds after she found out. Relieved, she wiped her forehead.

The doorbell rang. She hung up the phone and went to greet her grandmother.

Throughout the day with Mama Bliss, Charlie's mind swarmed with ways the deception could explode in her face. Uncle Ben could call while she was sitting here shellacking Christmas bottles and talk to Mama. Or Daddy! He could be calling right now! What if Sienna picked up the phone and he told her? How could she get packed and ready with everybody home? What if somebody got sick and stayed home on Friday? What if—

"Charlie! Where's your brain? Hand me some more tape," Mama Bliss said.

Charlie obeyed.

"You still upset about that oratory contest? Too bad. But don't go blaming your father. Like I say, don't go looking where you fell, but examine where you first slipped." The old woman returned to her work.

In the corner of the room stood a row of Christmas bottles painted in shades of red, white, and green. Mama Bliss had decorated each with Christmas symbols: doves of peace, bells, snowmen, gifts, trees, ornaments, and glued bits of brightly colored sequins that caught the light. The sight of the completed bottles reminded Charlie of the Winter Holiday Bazaar.

"Mama Bliss, I forgot to ask you something. Would you give me some of your Christmas bottles to sell at our bazaar? I'd help with the taping and painting," said Charlie. "The money will go to feed the hungry people in Africa. Plus we'll make ten percent profit."

"Why didn't you tell me earlier? You know I have orders to fill!" snapped her grandmother. "Only if you work hard with me. How about next weekend? We can get a dozen or two done."

"I can't!" Then, seeing a suspicious, squinty look in her grandmother's eyes, Charlie said, "I mean, I'll change my plans. Sure, next weekend is fine."

"Hmm. I smell a dead cat on the line."

Charlie glued her eyes to the bottle in her hands.

By the time Mama Bliss dropped her back home, Charlie's stomach was a web of rubber bands, snapping back and forth. Why had she ever lied in the first place? What could she do now? Call Uncle Ben and tell him the truth? Yes. But she couldn't dial the phone number.

The rest of the afternoon and part of the evening Charlie spent shopping with her mother. She felt miserable, though. And on Sunday she felt worse. Each time the telephone rang, Charlie leaped up to catch it first. Luckily, Uncle Ben did not call. Joshua. Saundra, twice. Granddad. Katie Rose.

By Monday morning, Charlie was a nervous wreck. She could hardly wait to tell Katie Rose at lunch.

After they'd swapped lunches, more now from habit, Charlie talked as Katie Rose's eyes widened and her mouth opened in amazement. "Charlie, you've got to stop this! Your father will kill you if you get on that airplane! Just call your uncle and explain it to him, just like you did to me," she pleaded. "He'll understand."

"But I really have to go to Washington, D.C., with him "

"Bad enough to face your father when you get off that plane on Sunday evening? Nothing is worth that, Charlie," she said.

"There has to be some way I can go without my parents finding out," Charlie said.

"How? Even if you told your parents you were spending

the weekend with me, your uncle would say something, or your aunt would." Katie Rose shook her head, her face grim. "No, Charlie, there is no way you can get away with this one. No way."

"That's a brilliant idea! I'll tell them I'm spending the weekend with you. I'll have to call Mama Bliss and tell her," Charlie said, biting into a tart green apple.

"You're fooling yourself because you want to go so much. Charlie, I'm your friend. Right?" asked Katie Rose. Charlie nodded.

"Then watch my lips. Your father will send you to Siberia for this one!"

"Will you help me?" Charlie persisted.

Katie Rose nodded. "I owe you, Charlie, for not doing detention. Coward that I am, I'll help you. But you have to promise me one thing."

"What?"

"When your father finds out, and he will, you must agree to torture and eternal detention before you let him know that I was involved." Katie Rose was so serious that her blue eyes looked slate gray.

"I'll do my best," vowed Charlie.

Monday night Charlie hovered by the telephone, but her uncle didn't call. By Wednesday her mother was making jokes about her having a boyfriend like Sienna. Charlie was grateful that Sienna was too wrapped up in her own problems to notice. Daddy was busy working overtime.

That night she called her grandmother, saying that she'd forgotten about spending the weekend with Katie Rose. From the clucks on the other end of the line, she knew that Mama Bliss had doubts. And later, when her parents were watching TV and Sienna was in the bathtub, she called her uncle.

Thursday turned into a whirlwind day. She and Katie Rose put up the last of the posters around the school while Chris announced the bazaar over the office intercom for the third time. Stacks of items cluttered the back of the classroom. Charlie helped her teacher organize the chaos. After school, she went to detention.

The telephone didn't ring the entire evening. Charlie perched on the edge of a chair in the kitchen, ready to run for the phone. Even Popcorn was jumpy.

"Charlie, are you getting sick? Here, let me feel your forehead." Her mother sat down next to her. "You've been acting strange. Are you unhappy about not being able to go to Washington, D.C., with your uncle?"

"No, Mama, I feel fine," replied Charlie, trying to appear normal.

"Maybe you should call Katie Rose and tell her you can't stay over this weekend."

"Oh, no, Mama. I have to go! I mean, we made special plans."

"Then you get to bed early tonight," said her mother.

When Charlie was convinced that Sienna was dead to the world, she got up and tiptoed about the room from bed to closet to drawer with the lightness of a ghost. Soon her suitcase was full and hidden again. Charlie eased into bed next to Popcorn. In a few hours Uncle Ben would knock on the front door.

Fifteen

The alarm clock buzzed. Seven o'clock! Sienna's bed was empty and the chatter from the rest of the house alerted Charlie that her parents were up. She pretended to be asleep so that by the time Mama called her, she was late enough to be the last to leave the house. By 7:45 A.M., everyone was out the door!

Charlie rushed to change into wool slacks and a sweater, and grabbed her heavy winter coat and the suitcase. She checked to make sure that Popcorn had fresh water and a full bowl of food. Sheba prowled behind her.

The weather forecaster promised rain during the weekend. Uncle Ben had told her that there was a light snow in Washington, D.C., so Charlie put on her boots. Right then the door buzzer rang twice. She peeked through the window. Singing, he came in. Charlie felt guiltier. He really trusted her, just as Mama and Daddy did. But it was too late now.

As she locked the front door, Charlie gasped. "Uncle Ben, I forgot to do something! I'll be back in one second. Promise!" she called. She ran to her bedroom. There, in plain sight, was the purple bookbag, sitting on top of her desk. With one fierce boot, she shoved it way under the bed and raced back down the hall.

They were in the middle of traffic headed for Oakland Airport when Charlie frowned. She'd forgotten something else. The *National Geographic* magazine was packed in her suitcase. But the newspaper article with the names of her father's dead friends was not with the Vietnam buttons in her sweater pocket. She must have left it in her jeans pocket.

At least she knew the men's names: Gerald Moer and Fred Hansen. And she remembered the day they died. Charlie grabbed her purse and wrote down the names and date.

There was no need to check their small bags at the airport. Uncle Ben told her they would be changing planes in Chicago. They would have less than half an hour to make the next flight.

By the time they landed in Chicago, Charlie's fears had subsided. Together she and Uncle Ben hurried down the terminal to the next gate to catch the plane that would take them from Chicago to the nation's capital. Huffing, they arrived in time.

Charlie clutched Uncle Ben's hand when the plane bumped down onto the runway at National Airport. Aunt Jessie was there. Her mother's oldest sister was a sweet-faced, dimpled woman who had no children.

"What in the world is going on? I must be seeing an apparition! This can't be Charlie!" she exclaimed. "You're really here, just like you promised! Come here, child, and let me hug you! Ben, you devil, you!"

Uncle Ben grinned good-naturedly, letting his sister jab him in the side for fooling her. Aunt Jessie hugged and kissed Charlie, stepping back to pinch Ben.

From family photographs, Charlie knew that her aunt lived in a brick house. On the way there, Aunt Jessie bombarded her with questions. When she said, "As soon as we get home, we'll call your mother to let her know that you got in," Charlie almost lost her lunch. That she hadn't thought of.

Lying again, Charlie said, "Nobody's home. They went out to dinner and to a show. Call tomorrow, Aunt Jessie."

"No. Knowing Oscar, we'd better call no matter how late it gets. Right, Ben? It's miracle enough that he let you come, Charlie. Honey, you warm enough? I know that your California weather is a lot friendlier."

Charlie lied once more and said she was really warm. Knowing that before the night ended she would have to tell Uncle Ben and Aunt Jessie the truth gave her the chills. What would they do? Ship her back on the first plane?

Outside Charlie saw large buildings, statues, and wide avenues that curved. Every now and then, Aunt Jessie pointed out some sight concealed in the shadows. Finally, her aunt parked the car on Newport Place, a street in the northwest section of the city. Charlie's head throbbed.

Her first impression of the house was one of light and color. The walls were a warm white and covered with artwork. Track lights ran across the ceiling, illuminating the bold abstract paintings. Elegant wooden statues reigned on tabletops and mantels. And the yellow rug and semicircular modular sofa created an ambience of comfort and beauty.

Aunt Jessie sure knows how to live, Charlie thought, as she was directed to a small room in the back of the house. It was one of three bedrooms. Her aunt had a good job in the post office. That plus a generous divorce settlement some years ago had left her in secure economic shape.

After getting settled, Charlie joined her relatives. Aunt Jessie had prepared food and drinks. She handed her niece a cup of hot chocolate with marshmallows floating on top.

"Well, I'd better call Ellie and Oscar before we get too relaxed and forget." She smiled.

Startled, Charlie jumped up, spilling some of the drink on her sweater. "No, Aunt Jessie! No one's home!"

"Honey, if they're not home yet, we'll know. I really don't want Oscar worried. He'll never allow you to come again if I don't call." She began to push the buttons.

"Aunt Jessie, you can't call!" Tripping over Uncle Ben's legs, Charlie ran over to her.

"I don't understand. What's the matter, Charlie?" Aunt Jessie asked, holding the receiver in her hand.

Charlie looked from her aunt's concerned face to her uncle's puzzled one. By now he had put down his drink and was studying her.

"Oh, Charlie, you didn't?" he said.

Aunt Jessie hung up the telephone. "Didn't what, Ben? I don't understand."

Charlie collapsed into the rocking chair near the sofa.

"Didn't what, Ben? Charlie?" Aunt Jessie repeated, standing there with her right hand on her hip, wearing that expression that told Charlie she, like Mama Bliss, also smelled a dead cat on the line.

Uncle Ben groaned and took a long drink from the tall glass. "You tell her, Charlie."

Charlie wanted to sneak away. Part of her had suspected that she would get caught, but she'd had no idea it would feel this awful.

"I lied." Charlie stopped. Those words tasted worse than the cod liver oil Mama had made her take when she was a toddler. "I lied to Daddy and Mama and Mama Bliss. And I lied to you, Uncle Ben, when I told you they gave me permission to come." Then she added, "Here."

Aunt Jessie threw up her hands. "Oh, Lord, you mean that Ellie and Oscar don't know you're here! In Washington!"

Charlie bowed her head. The chances of getting out of this mess without confronting her parents were zero. She could tell by the solemn expression on her uncle's face. Katie Rose had been right.

"Why, Charlie?" Uncle Ben's voice sounded weary.

Fears dammed up, then flooded out. Between sobs and hiccups, she tried to explain. "I wanted to come. Daddy said I couldn't, because it wasn't the best time. But I've been so good at school and at home. And I have to see the Memorial and bring Daddy a gift. And this is the only time I know."

The sound of Aunt Jessie's rich laughter shocked both of them. Clutching the side of the couch, she was laughing so hard she couldn't stand erect. "Oscar will have a heart attack," she gasped out. "Lord. Lord." Then she fell on the couch, holding her sides. When she'd composed herself, she said, "Child! How did you ever have the nerve to pull a stunt like this?"

Charlie couldn't answer, because she didn't know. She just felt she'd had to come.

"Charlie, where do Oscar and Ellie think you are at this minute?" Ben asked, without the hint of a smile.

"With my girlfriend Katie Rose Bainbridge, spending the weekend." Charlie wiped at her eyes. "But you can't mention her name. I promised her I'd never let Daddy find out she was involved."

Uncle Ben stood up. "Oscar is never going to believe that I didn't have some part in this. Well, no sense sending you back home. We're leaving day after tomorrow, anyway. I am so disappointed in you."

"Well, brother, what do we do now?" asked Aunt Jessie.

"Charlie, you know what you have to do. Don't you?" he replied.

Charlie rose and walked to the telephone. Her mother answered. Charlie told her that she was in Washington, D.C., at her Aunt Jessie's with Uncle Ben. There was a long, incredulous silence.

Repeating the same message to her father was harder because her voice quaked. His silence was shorter.

Minutes later, she handed the phone to her uncle, listening as he explained what had happened and gave her father their flight number and arrival time on Sunday evening. Then Aunt Jessie got on the phone and talked to her sister. All the while Charlie thought about what her father had said, the angry sputters and the threats.

Aunt Jessie turned on the stereo. "That's over and you're here, Chartreuse Marie Pippin. So let's make the best of this visit. Ben, can I freshen your drink?"

But Uncle Ben wasn't ready to put it behind them. "Charlie, don't you ever lie to me again. That's all I have

159

to say. No matter what happens." His scarred hands rested heavily on her shoulders. She had to bend back to see him.

"I'm sorry, Uncle Ben. I was wrong," Charlie cried.

"Right. You were wrong." He walked away.

Before Charlie climbed into bed, she made a second futile search for the newspaper article about her father. At least she'd remembered what she needed. Exhausted, she pulled the covers over her head.

Charlie awoke early and jumped out of bed. She looked in on her aunt. Aunt Jessie slept on her back, her arms crossed and her head to one side. Uncle Ben's door was shut.

On an impulse Charlie flung her arms wide and whirled around. "I'm here! Really here!" she whispered, feeling a secret thrill. While she waited for the day to start, she folded an origami crane and a red flower with a stem.

After breakfast, everyone dressed. Uncle Ben had a friend he wanted to see that afternoon, and Charlie was to go shopping and sightseeing with her aunt. But that morning they drove to the Vietnam Memorial.

The weather was colder than in California, so Aunt Jessie provided Charlie with a warm hat and gloves. And a camera. In the rush, she'd forgotten that, too. Charlie carried the magazine and her notepad. She wanted to remember everything!

The moment Aunt Jessie had parked, Charlie leaped eagerly from the car. Ahead of her, on a mound of winter grass, Charlie saw a tent, a stand, a sign, and flags flapping in the wind. Blown-up photographs of men were hung on wooden racks near the flags. She walked over and read the large sign: VETERAN'S VIGIL OF HONOR. Below that were the words *You are an American. Your voice can make the difference.* Charlie recognized the initials POW MIA. Prisoners of War. Missing in Action. Then she saw pamphlets, buttons, and other items about POWs and MIAs at the stand.

"Uncle Ben, that stands for the soldiers some people believe are in prison in Vietnam or dead, but the Vietnam government won't give us back their bodies. Right?" she asked, snapping two pictures.

He nodded. "Charlie, please don't take any of me. I don't feel like posing for pictures today."

"Okay, I won't."

"Ben, you want to go on? Charlie and I will wait for you," said Aunt Jessie.

He nodded again. Charlie recognized the distant, mournful expression in his eyes. She knew he had friends on the wall, just as Daddy did.

"Sure, Jess. This is something I have to do." He started walking up the mound to a path to the left.

"Charlie, let him alone," Aunt Jessie said.

"No, Aunt Jessie. I have to go, too!" And Charlie ran after her uncle, grabbing his hand. "That's why I came!" Her aunt followed.

There were other people on the long, curved path, some with small children. To her left, Charlie saw a Black family, the father, mother, and two children. One girl was about her age. An older white man huddled around a wooden stand. Charlie waited with her aunt and uncle while the family turned the pages of a book, then moved away. The elderly man did the same.

Charlie read the title of the large book, *Directory of Names*. From her research, she knew that in this book were the names of all of the women and men who had died or were listed as missing in action during the Vietnam War. That included the first deaths in 1959 and the last deaths in 1975. It was a thick book with many single-spaced pages.

Uncle Ben took a piece of crumpled paper out of his wallet. It looked as if it had been there a long time. The paper was so creased that he had to unfold it slowly.

Aunt Jessie showed her brother how to locate the names of the friends he was seeking. She reached into her purse and handed him a pen. After searching, his finger leading him, he paused, writing down a panel number and a line number. These would tell him exactly where on the 492-foot-long granite wall the names of the men he knew were engraved. Then he wrote down two more sets of numbers before giving Charlie the pen.

Charlie found Fred Hansen by the date of his death. Then Gerald Moer. She copied the numbers.

The pathway meandered through a parklike setting. Stark, bare trees lined both sides. There was light snowfall on the ground that crunched beneath her boots. Charlie had expected to see the wall immediately, but instead, the path led down a gradual incline. To her left, in the distance, she saw the grand spire of the Washington Monument.

At last they reached one end of the wall. Charlie remembered that the Vietnam Memorial wall was made of polished black granite. It was V-shaped, with one arm pointed toward the Washington Monument and the other arm aimed at the Lincoln Memorial. She was at the end of the wall that pointed toward the Washington Monument, which explained why she could see the tall spire. The long wall was divided into one hundred and fifty panels, each forty inches wide. On each panel were carved the names of the dead and missing in action. Charlie had to squat down to read the names on the panels at the end. That was because the panels decreased in height from the center of the wall, where they were almost eleven feet high, to the ends of the wall, where they were only eight inches high.

As the path proceeded downward, toward the center of the V, the panels got taller, until they towered above Charlie. She had to stare up to see the names at the top. The wall was like a huge wide V built into the earth, opening its arms in welcome, beckoning her to enter. The black granite panels were so highly polished that she could see her face in them.

Walking along the path, she saw small American flags stuck into the ground below. And taped to a panel was one red, shriveled rose.

The Vietnam Memorial was real. Real. Scary. Beautiful. Each time Charlie looked at a panel she saw her face, Uncle Ben, the naked trees and sky. In front of her, a woman paused. Her fingers ran down the wall, counting the small dots on the side of each panel that marked ten rows. Next to her a man and a little girl fidgeted. The child was watching the woman. Charlie heard her ask, "What is Mommy looking for, Papa?" And she heard him reply, "The name of someone she loves."

Uncle Ben stopped, his eyes sweeping the panel numbers and letters. "Rows and rows of names," Charlie heard him mutter, shaking his head. "Rows and rows." From her report, she knew how many names were cut into the stone that had been quarried not far from Bangalore, India—58,007 names.

While Uncle Ben's hand searched, Charlie watched. Then, as if a cold wind had swept over him, she saw his body begin to tremble. His fingers touched the letters of a name. Afraid, Charlie stood there, wishing that her aunt were closer. But Aunt Jessie was talking to the couple with the little girl.

His hand moved again, this time down and to the left. It stopped, and this time he froze. Charlie couldn't see her uncle's face. There were other people around them. He stood there a long time. Finally, she touched his arm. Clearly she saw the two of them and the snow on the ground and the dull, cold sky and the faded red rose. And she saw tears streaming down her uncle's face.

He reached out and held her close, his eyes never leaving the panel. Charlie looked up at him. And she knew that he didn't see her. For a second she thought she was standing there with her father, holding him while he cried.

"Were they your best friends, too, Uncle Ben?" she whispered, thinking of Gerald Moer and Fred Hansen. She had to repeat the question twice before he heard her.

"They were my men," he said. He wiped at his face with his free hand, sniffing. From the way he held his body, Charlie realized that he wanted to stay, so she gently disengaged herself. She had work to do.

A few panels down she discovered the names she sought: Gerald Moer and Fred Hansen. One name was too high for her to touch, but she could see it. Charlie faced her panel.

"Hi, I'm Charlie, Oscar Pippin's daughter," she whispered. "I came to see you. My daddy is fine. I know he still misses you." She took a deep breath and squeezed back the tears. This was not the time to cry. Then she saw the person she needed, the park ranger.

"Mister," Charlie asked, "please make a rubbing of two names for me."

The white-haired man ambled over and took a pencil and two strips of white paper out of his coat pocket. Charlie pointed to the names and repeated them while he laid a piece of white paper over each name. Next, he rubbed the pencil over the raised letters underneath the paper. He handed her the first strip, then started on the second. Charlie stared at the elegant, engraved letters. She thanked the ranger when he handed her the second strip. He moved on to help someone else.

With care, Charlie took the origami flower out of her pocket and wedged the stem into the slight break in the panel midway between the two names. "For you two to remember me and Daddy," she whispered. "And for us to remember you, Fred Hansen and Gerald Moer." Then Charlie bent her head and said a prayer, letting the tears fall. Moments later, she composed herself and took several photographs, making sure to get their names.

"Charlie, you ready? It's getting cold out here," her aunt called. Charlie looked around for her uncle. He was still where she'd left him. Holding the strips carefully in one hand, she reached into her pocket.

"Here, Uncle Ben," she said, going up to him and handing him the origami crane she'd made that morning and the tape she'd grabbed from Aunt Jessie's desk before they left. "I made this."

Charlie held her breath, hoping that he would accept the golden crane. The crane was one of the most difficult origami figures to fold, and the wings weren't quite straight. Maybe he wouldn't notice, she thought.

"The crane is a symbol of peace," she added. "You can tape it to the wall. Like the rose down there."

Smiling a little, he took the golden crane while Charlie tore off a piece of Scotch tape. Then he taped the paper bird to the wall and stepped back.

Against the black mirror, the gold paper shone even brighter. Charlie smiled. Uncle Ben had stopped crying. She reached for his hand and squeezed hard.

"Ben, you ready?" Aunt Jessie asked, handing him a Kleenex from her purse.

"Thanks, Jessie, I'm ready," he said, straightening and blowing his nose.

"My, what a beautiful bird!" Aunt Jessie said.

"Our niece made that crane, Jessie." There was pride in his voice. "Will they throw it away?" he asked.

"Oh, no, Uncle Ben. I read an article that said the rangers collect the things people leave at the Vietnam Memorial and keep them in a special storage room. They even wear gloves when they pick them up," Charlie said.

By now they were walking up an incline, past the other arm of the V that formed the wall, toward the second Vietnam Memorial, a statue of three infantrymen. Charlie looked back to photograph the panels once more. She wondered why the Vietnam Memorial had been called such horrible names. She recalled reading that some said it was "ugly," "a black wound," and "a shameful grave." Charlie thought there was something right about a memorial that honored, name by name, every American who had died or was missing in action. She liked the idea of placing the panels in the earth, but visible to the living eye and open to the air and the sky.

Charlie thought Maya Lin had done a great job. She was the young Chinese-American student whose design was selected for the memorial. Charlie had read that she got a *B* from her teacher on this project. *That* showed that grades weren't everything. She should have gotten an *A!* And it had been wise not to place the memorial in a desolate place, but instead in the nation's capital, surrounded by its most revered historical architecture. Reluctantly, she joined her uncle and aunt by the bronze statue, only yards away from the wall.

"So many names," Uncle Ben murmured to himself, staring back.

Aunt Jessie whirled around. "That's most of the men of my generation on that wall! And too many sent home torn up, on drugs, or with their hearts and minds messed up! What good are memorials when so many of them need medical help and jobs today? Tell me, Ben!"

Aunt Jessie's bitterness startled Charlie. Gone was the laughter, replaced by anger and sorrow. What surprised Charlie was that Mama never talked like that. Mama just loved Daddy and tried to hold the family together. For the first time, Charlie wondered if her mother shared any of Aunt Jessie's feelings.

Uncle Ben sighed and kissed his sister's cheek. Then

he took her arm. "Calm down, Jess. I came home. So did Oscar. A lot of us survived."

Charlie wanted to point back to the wall and say, "They didn't." She remembered her family's happy Thanksgiving dinner. And she thought that for every name on the wall there had been an empty space at some family's table.

Her aunt and uncle were examining the large bronze sculpture of three infantrymen. Together, they faced the Vietnam Memorial wall. One Black, one Hispanic, one Caucasian.

Charlie stared at the Black soldier. He did resemble her father in the old photograph. The same high cheekbones, full upper lip, and small ears set close to his head. In his right hand was a helmet and in his left, a large rifle. Even the veins in his arms stood out as her father's did. She noticed that the sculptor, Frederick Hart, had placed the three men close, so they touched. Charlie liked that. She took more pictures.

At the base of the statue, someone had left a bouquet of red, white, and blue carnations with a white ribbon that said, "Our son, Jose." She handed the camera to her aunt. Digging in her purse, Charlie took out the buttons, NO MORE VIETNAMS and WELCOME HOME, VIETNAM VETS. Kneeling down, Charlie laid the buttons at the base of the statue. She had finished what she had come to do.

They stopped at the souvenir shop, where Charlie bought a keychain with a picture of the Vietnam Memorial on it for Katie Rose, a comb and mirror set for her mother, and postcards for everyone else. Uncle Ben didn't buy anything.

Charlie was grateful when her aunt suggested that they

get a quick snack at the refreshment stand before making the long climb to the Lincoln Memorial. From there Uncle Ben caught a cab to visit friends, while she and Aunt Jessie toured the National Archives and the National Art Gallery, then stopped for a chocolate milkshake at a Hot Shoppe on Georgia Avenue. Over their milkshakes, Aunt Jessie promised to get the film developed and mail Charlie the photographs.

Once home at Aunt Jessie's, Charlie laid the rubbings between the pages of a magazine. The trip was over. Tomorrow they would leave for Berkeley. Alone in the cozy bedroom, Charlie wondered what her father was going to do to her.

Sixteen

Buckled in, bound for Oakland Airport, Charlie felt as mixed up as a set of alphabet letters in a toy box. The experiences of the short weekend flooded her mind. She leaned on the armrest and stared out the window.

"Charlie, what's wrong?" Uncle Ben asked.

She leaned back. "I thought going with you would be so exciting. So much fun! Some of the trip was. But seeing the wall and the statue . . . All those names were real people. Like you. Like Daddy. I feel . . ." The words trailed off.

"I hope I didn't upset you, crying yesterday?" He held her hand.

"I cried, too." Charlie's thoughts shifted to home. "Mama said you might marry Dinah."

"I love her. Marrying Dinah and having a family sound good to me. You'll like her, Charlie. You'll see."

"I want you and Dinah to be real happy." Charlie paused. "If you love her, I know I'll like her. Mama says Dinah is good for you. It was nice of her to get me such a low plane fare, Uncle Ben."

"When we get home, I'm going to stay and talk to Oscar, Charlie. I know what you did was wrong," he said. "I probably shouldn't have invited you in the middle of the school year." He smiled.

"Thanks, Uncle Ben. Anything you can do to keep Daddy from killing me, I'd appreciate. And I never said how sorry I felt for getting you involved in my Halloween business. In case Daddy sends me to Siberia, I also want you to know I'll be happy to come to your wedding."

Uncle Ben kissed Charlie on the cheek.

Charlie spotted her family in the crowd of people waiting at the airport gate. Her father, first. Then Mama and Sienna. The rain fell steadily in dark sheets.

Her father's eyes locked into hers like radar finding its target. The nearer she got, the harder it was to look at him. As usual, Mama maneuvered her body between Charlie and her father.

"Hi, Mama, Sienna, and Daddy," said Charlie. Her head started to swim and she tottered in her mother's arms.

"Now, you keep quiet, no matter what your father says," her mother whispered in her ear. Charlie peeked over her mother's shoulder to see Daddy fold his arms across the breadth of his chest.

"Well, Miss Pippin, now that you are grown enough to lie to us, disobey us, disturb the order in our home, get on a plane without our permission, I guess you're grown enough to take care of yourself," he growled at her.

"Oh, Daddy, you promised Mama no arguing in public," said Sienna, blowing her nose.

One glower shut Sienna up. In her head Charlie ticked

off the list of things her father could do to her. The first category was physical harm, ranging from abuse to murder. But he wouldn't do that. Mama would stop him from hitting her.

The second category included screaming at her or putting her on some form of punishment. The final one was labeled Siberia. He could send her away to live somewhere. She didn't think Mama would allow that, either.

"Come on, Oscar, Charlie. Hey, Ben, want to come over to the house? Sienna, help your sister with that bag." Mrs. Pippin directed the family with the natural command of a conductor.

Mutely, Charlie gazed at her uncle, praying that he would remember the promise he'd made to her on the airplane and not run off to see Dinah. They had a whole lifetime to hug and kiss! Whereas Charlie might not even live through the night! She walked several steps behind her father, near Sienna.

"Charlie, you should have seen Daddy's face when he found out that you'd gone with Uncle Ben." Sienna moved slowly, increasing the distance. "I thought he was going to burst a blood vessel!"

"Did he say anything?" asked Charlie.

"Are you crazy? He never stopped hollering. Charlie, guess what? Mama had to get on the hotline and call Granddad and Mama Bliss." Sienna's eyes were shining as if she had a fever. "A royal family summit was convened! And your friend, Katie Rose, she sure stuck up for you. When Daddy called her, she kept saying you were there until he told her that he knew you were in Washington, D.C."

Charlie groaned. "Shoot, I promised not to get Katie Rose into trouble."

"You should have thought of that sooner. At least your pulling this insane stunt got Daddy's mind off me." Sienna grinned like the Cheshire cat. "Punishment or no punishment, I still see Joshua before school, during class breaks, at lunch, and for a few minutes after school."

But Charlie could have cared less about Sienna and Joshua. She was too preoccupied with the news about Katie Rose. The shoe was on her foot now. She was the one who would have to make things right between them.

Sienna pulled Charlie over. "Look, Joshua wants us to take tennis together next semester. That way we can practice together after school. I'm going to stop running with Daddy. I need you to take my place with him. I'll train you. Okay?"

Charlie glared at her sister in amazement. "Look, Sienna, I'm not your fill-in. I'll decide when and if I want to jog with Daddy. Don't you ever think about anybody but yourself?"

Mama and Uncle Ben maintained a steady stream of chatter in the car, not allowing a moment's silence. Charlie and Sienna ignored each other.

Charlie's father was the last person to enter the house, slamming the wooden door shut. Granddad and Mama Bliss were seated in front of the cold fireplace. Popcorn bounded over to jump on Charlie. The Christmas decorations were up.

"Hi, Granddad. Hi, Mama Bliss," said Charlie, going to kiss each of them, shrinking at the loud "harumph" from her tight-faced grandmother.

"So this is the jet-setter?" joked Granddad.

Mama Bliss scowled. "No, this is the rebel who lied to me!"

The family gathered around the dining room table. True to his word, Uncle Ben explained everything in a low-key manner.

"Charlie, what have you got to say for yourself? I swear I don't know who you think you are!" The punch of her father's words hurt. She flinched.

All eyes focused on her.

"Don't shush me, Ellie. The girl is wrong, and I want to know what made her do something like this. Charlie, tell me!" His fist pounded the table.

Charlie opened her mouth. She had to find her voice and say something. "Daddy, I was wrong. I mean, to lie to everyone. That wasn't right. And to get Katie Rose in trouble. That was bad, too." Charlie's eyes met her father's. "I wanted to go to Washington, D.C., to see the Vietnam Memorial. I had to go."

"Oh, Charlie, there would have been other trips," her mother said.

"No, there wouldn't, Mama. Not with Uncle Ben, not like this one. Would there?" Her eyes held her uncle's.

"No, Charlie," he admitted.

"Besides," she added, "I had to see the wall now. I mean, after writing my report and—and everything."

"You can't get what you want every time you think you want it," her father said.

"You have something else to say, don't you?" asked her grandfather, his hands folded before him on the table.

Charlie thought. "I wanted to see the Vietnam Memorial

and the statue," she repeated. This was not the time to speak of the rubbings.

"Well, I'm utterly speechless, Charlie," said Mama Bliss. "This trip of yours takes every rag off every bush for me!"

"I'm not speechless!" Daddy thundered. "Call Mr. and Mrs. Bainbridge and apologize for your behavior. And I want you to apologize to every person at this table for lying! I'll decide what your punishment is later. But you can bet it will be severe."

Charlie obeyed. She completed all of her apologies, called Katie Rose and spoke to both of her parents. That took two phone calls.

Soon after, Uncle Ben gave her a kiss and left to see Dinah. It was a relief to escape to the bedroom. But she'd hardly sat on the bed when she heard a light knock at the door. Charlie opened it.

Granddad walked in and sat down next to her. "Why didn't you tell your father what you learned going to see the Memorial, Charlie?"

"I couldn't. See what I got for Daddy? These are his friends. I read that you could get rubbings made. Wait a minute, let me double-check the newspaper article." Her jeans were hanging on the back of the chair. Carefully, she slid the article out. "Yes! I got the names and date exactly right!"

"These are very powerful, aren't they, Charlie?" He handed them back to her.

She nodded.

On Monday morning, Charlie waited in the rain for Katie Rose to get off the yellow school bus. In her pants pocket was the keychain she'd bought for Katie Rose at the Memorial. The materials to make origami figures filled her bookbag, along with a list of the afternoons she was due at Mama Bliss's, after detention, to tape Christmas bottles.

"Hi, runaway," teased Katie Rose. She was wearing her orange rain slicker and bright red boots.

"Hi, Katie Rose. Did I get you in a whole lot of trouble with your parents?"

"Let's get inside!"

It wasn't until they were at the cluster that Katie Rose answered Charlie's last question.

"Yes, my parents got upset. But they're always upset, and I decided not to let them drive me crazy." She grinned. "Charlie, we're friends. I owed you one for the Halloween business. So now we're even."

"That makes me feel better. When did you get your hair cut?" asked Charlie, noticing that Katie Rose's hair was short, with a longer section hanging over the right side of her face. She looked older.

"You like it? I do. On Saturday, I went up to Telegraph Avenue, near the university, and got it cut." Katie Rose grinned.

"What did your parents do?" Charlie asked.

"Got upset." The two friends laughed.

When Katie Rose asked her about the trip, Charlie hesitated. She wasn't ready to talk about what she had seen.

But Charlie had to face Mrs. Hayamoto. She told her the real reason for her absence on Friday. Then she saw the discipline points she'd earned erased. Once more her name was entered at the bottom of the chart. Charlie sighed, resigned to figuring out a way to move up. Again.

Already she had one idea. She could donate her 10 percent of the profits from the Winter Holiday Bazaar to the fund. Mrs. Hayamoto had gotten permission from Mr. Rocker to offer points to encourage the spirit of giving. Those points plus the ones she could earn for the extra work she was doing for the bazaar could move her up three slots. She would have to think about this.

At this time, the trip to Disneyland seemed out of reach, but at least she could get off the bottom of the list.

During lunch, the former war and peace committee worked in the room, preparing for the bazaar that Friday. Chris struggled with a crane. Finally, Charlie showed him how to make a dove. They decided to charge more for cranes. Katie Rose had mastered both forms.

Suddenly, Charlie hurried over to the supply table.

"What's the matter?" Chris asked.

"I have a great money-making idea!" Charlie grabbed a hole puncher and a piece of yarn. "Look, you two! We can sell tons of these at the bazaar."

Charlie held up a silver origami crane, dangling from the piece of yarn.

"Now that is real ingenuity, Charlie." Chris shook his head.

"A Christmas tree ornament!" Katie Rose beamed.

"We can market them as peace-tree ornaments, Chris. Customers can hang these on their trees, even their plants, and have an instant peace tree." Charlie talked so fast she stuttered.

"People could hang them in backyards. On the trees in

their neighborhoods. All over the world!" Katie Rose started dancing around.

"That's a lot of birds," Chris said, taking out his calculator. "And what do we do about the rain? They need to be waterproofed if they hang outside."

"I'll come up with something to solve that," Charlie said, folding another crane. "We can make this idea work. Right?"

"Right." Chris and Katie Rose agreed to make as many as they could before the bazaar.

Late that night Charlie woke up starving. A box of cranes and doves rested on her desk next to a small stack of handpainted cards. She was getting a late start, with Christmas only a week and a half away. She had folded and painted for hours, skipping dinner.

Charlie climbed out of bed. Her robe was flung on the chair right below the third-place ribbon she'd Scotchtaped to her bookshelf.

Sienna's snores were gurgly from the cold. Charlie felt under her bed for her slippers. Her hand brushed against the change box and the briefcase. The rain had stopped. Popcorn stirred.

The house was silent. When Charlie saw a light under the kitchen door, she figured that someone had forgotten to turn it off. But after she pushed the door open, she saw her father eating a piece of cake.

"Don't just stand there. Come in here."

"Hi, Daddy. I got hungry," she said, ready to bolt.

"Then eat." He returned to the science fiction book before him.

Charlie threw together a cheese sandwich, grabbed an apple, and poured a glass of milk. She sat at the side of the table, near the kitchen window.

He closed the book. "I never heard of any kid pulling a stunt like that." He shook his head. "I still can't believe you actually went."

The kitchen was so quiet that when Charlie sipped her milk she thought that the sound might wake her sister.

"I've been considering pulling you out of Hayden or transferring you to another room," he said.

The very idea of leaving her friends and the familiar routine of Mrs. Hayamoto's class horrified her. Would Daddy really move her? One look at his set face told her the truth.

"Your mother disagrees. I don't know what to do with you. I still don't understand why you had to go, Charlie. Why?"

Charlie realized that Daddy was waiting for her to answer, but not in his familiar tense, angry way. He was waiting quietly, as if he really wanted to understand. But how could she explain what had propelled her to the Vietnam Memorial? Raking so many faces, voices, facts, photographs, and feelings into neat piles like fallen September leaves was beyond her. She sighed, a deep, heartfelt sigh.

"Just a minute, Daddy," she said at last. Charlie rose, left, and returned. In her hands were the two rubbings. She laid them gently on the kitchen table before him. He moved his head from one to the other. She noticed that his thick fingers brushed over Gerald Moer's name the way Uncle Ben's had touched the wall. With a slight, wry smile he did the same with Fred Hansen's rubbing.

Then he looked up. "You've seen the old newspaper clipping?"

"Yes, Daddy," she said, perching on one foot. The article was in an envelope she'd mailed to Mama Bliss, enclosed in a handpainted thank-you card. Back where it belonged.

"These rubbings came from the wall?" he asked.

Charlie lowered herself into the chair. "Yes, Daddy."

"Once upon a time and only yesterday . . ." He ran his hand over them. "This is part of why you went, Charlie?"

"I found the article about you being a decorated Vietnam hero by accident in one of Mama Bliss's old albums. But even before that I wanted to learn about the war because of you. So I decided to study it for school. That's how I found out about the wall in Washington, D.C., and the rubbings. When Uncle Ben called, I had to go." She could feel her heart pounding.

"The three of us were like brothers. . . . We had this pact to make it home. Together. . . ."

Charlie waited. They were having their first real conversation, where one person talks and the other listens. Taking turns.

"You're still wrong for going and lying, Charlie." She watched as he pointed to the rubbings. "This doesn't change that. You're still on punishment."

Sitting straight in her chair, Charlie nodded, hands clasped together on the table. She stared at the green stone in her ring.

He picked up the white strips of paper. "What did you think giving these to me would do? Get you out of trouble?"

"No, Daddy. I thought—I mean, I hoped they would help you feel better." Charlie spoke slowly, feeling her way. "I talked to your friends. To their names on the panel. I told them that I was your daughter and that you still missed them." She stopped, then lifted her head higher. "I left a red origami flower by their names."

The fading darkness outside hung as light as a cashmere cloak around the house. Charlie saw tears in her father's eyes. He twisted around to stare out the window in the direction of the star rock. When he turned back, he wiped his eyes with his hands.

"Charlie Pippin," he said, shaking his head.

A look passed between them. Charlie met his eyes and said, "Daddy, I know."

His hand reached out and rested on her arm. "Thank you, Charlie, for these."

She placed her hand over his.

"You are some kind of daughter for a man like me to have," he said.

Charlie grinned. "One of a kind."

At that moment Charlie remembered the words her grandfather had spoken the afternoon when she had wanted to know about her father's old dreams. Like children, he had said, dreams are private. Then he'd told her to ask Daddy, but she had been too afraid. She wasn't now.

"Daddy, when you and Mama were young and dreamed about owning an inn on the Oregon coast, she said she would have written poetry there. But she wouldn't tell me what you'd wanted to do."

He let go of her arm to touch the edges of the rubbings.

She kept still. If dreams were private, Daddy had the right not to tell her.

But he did. "I would have painted."

Charlie wondered why she hadn't thought of that. After all, she and Sienna were named after colors. Mama Bliss painted. She painted, too! But there hadn't been any concrete clues to lead her to the discovery that Daddy's dream had been to be an artist. No talk about art school. No art supplies. No visits to art galleries. No paintings by her father on the walls.

"I bet you were good. Very good. Did you ever paint me, Daddy?"

He stared at the names again, then laid them down. "I did an oil portrait of you. You were learning to walk."

"Where is it?"

"I made your mother store it away." He passed a hand across his face as if removing a veil.

Then, he placed the rubbings in the science fiction book and rose, clearing the table.

Charlie carried her glass over to the sink. Side by side, they looked out. Now the backyard shimmered with light and glistened with dew. The good night had done its work.

Charlie dared one more question. "Can I see the painting you did of me?"

She heard her father reply, "Yes, one day."

And Charlie Pippin smiled.